Secret Hours

Mich

in

Harry O. Morris

Jason C. Eckhardt

&

Thomas Brown

with an introduction by

Robert M. Price

MYTHOS BOOKS LLC

POPLAR BLUFF

MISSOURI

2007

Mythos Books LLC
351 Lake Ridge Road,
Poplar Bluff,
MO 63901
United States of America

www.mythosbooks.com

Published by Mythos Books LLC 2007

FIRST EDITION

ISBN 0-9789911-0-9

Set in *Broken15* & *Adobe Garamond Pro*.

Broken15 by Misprinted Type.
www.misprintedtype.com

Adobe Garamond Pro by Adobe Systems Incorporated.
www.adobe.com

Typesetting, layout and design by PAW.

CONTENTS

Introduction: The Dark Angel

My first acquaintance with Michael Cisco, a pretty dubious one, was a suggestion he sent in, nearly anonymously and out of the void, to *Crypt of Cthulhu*, as to the possible meaning of the name Abdul Alhazred as "son of the strangler." Years later, he favored me with a translation 'back' into Greek of the infamous couplet, "That is not dead which can eternal lie, and with strange aeons, even death may die." As one can see from this, the etymological work of his character *The Divinity Student* is near and dear to his heart. In other ways too, that character is largely autobiographical. Michael is easy to discern in a crowd of mortals. You can spot him, even on a hot August day, sporting a black overcoat and black clothes. His pleasantly round face is masked in its accents by a pair of steel-rimmed glasses, giving him something of the appearance of the Nazi interrogator from *Raiders of the Lost Ark*, though handsome.

Thus one may say of Cisco what the Crow Man in Thomas Ligotti's *Vastarien* says of the unnamed occult volume: it is not merely about the subject matter, but is simply to be identified with it. An ironic pose perhaps, and yet the real thing. I have the definite impression that his literary characters emulate their creator and not the other way around.

You know the dangers of seeking to describe color to a blind man, and yet trying to do so enables us to see colors better than our vision alone does the job, since we are forced to use other senses than the accustomed one in the effort. In the same way, one is tempted to characterize Michael's fiction by another means than just suggesting it be read. If pressed, and the current necessity so presses me, I would venture that his is the writing of infrared vision. You are standing in a cemetery at midnight when the only illumination is the silver shadows of the moon, and, given the territory, you are seeing the truth of the matter better than the noontide sun could show it. That is the world, and the idiom of the writing of the (D)arkangel Michael.

Again, there is a restraint about these tales which only points up the very great richness implicit in them. And part

ix

of that richness is the terrible sense that their reality is only slightly removed from the world of mundane observation, providing that what we observe there falls along the spectrum of the hushed-up, the unfortunate, the places where the veneer wears thin. In this we can see readily a kinship with Ramsey Campbell and his trench-coated degenerates who are more. But to say so is less a comparison than it is a vague waving in the direction of the literary landscape one might place Cisco in, if that matters. And of course, Tom Ligotti would not be very far away on that map, either. William F. Burroughs would have to be a neighbor as well. And now you, too, will be.

—Robert M. Price,
October 2006

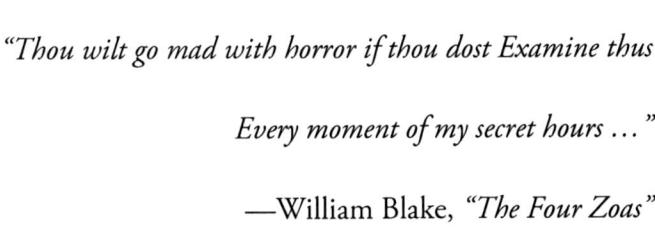

"Thou wilt go mad with horror if thou dost Examine thus

Every moment of my secret hours ..."

—William Blake, *"The Four Zoas"*

Two Fragments.

Tom Brown produced the art first, involving his acorn-headed, literal stick-figures, and asked me for some accompanying text. In the second of these two texts, I attempted to produce something approximating the fairy grammar of these creatures, which would consist almost exclusively of verb participates suggesting a series of states of activity.

Two Fragments

From the *Fornicati Daemonorum* of Master Flandus Null à Wallachia [c. 1600–1680s]—written at the court of Queen Cristina, of Sweden.

"… here … are also these wood-sprites, who are man-sized in their own proper forested places but of much smaller stature when very drolly visiting human persons. They are brought to the door with the promise of a handsome repast of pot-ash and small cups of turpentine, consuming it through the apertures of their eyes or by rubbing what they may get upon themselves and in some way absorbing it, as they have no mouths. In my father's laboratory our specimen also showed considerable inclination to phosphorus. This sprite we had captured and examined at our leisure. The head was found to be wholly empty, and this was no obstacle to the sensible behavior of this one."

[However, Sir Thomas Brown, in his *Vulgar Errors*, disputes Master Null, saying in brief: "… the sprite we had found exhibited within its acorn-head a minute and harmless worm which tapped against the walls of its enclosure and thereby produced an irregular rapping that we took for what passed for speech among them, and were assured that all of its kind were in this way identical, against the claims of the renowned Master Null …"]

"Those persons most familiar with the wood-sprites, having had many dealings with them, gave them this character: that they were silent and harmless, although among some there was known a "sprite's evil," which was a greatly accelerating growing of the hair and nails of some person, and the hair and nails thus grown would become uncuttably tough, and remain so, and this was taken as a sign of the sprite's displeasure; these sprites, in return for pot ash, would sometimes be cajoled to weave themselves together, being almost entirely like sticks, but these weavings being too brittle for use as anything, and the sprites being unwilling to remain long woven together or made into traps or baskets, this was of no use to anyone; these sprites whose heads were acorns would sometimes appear with walnut or chestnut headed cousins; they are repelled by fire and have a horror of fish, and these spirits and the toads are enemies; they value the holly berries, and, in their war with the toads, are allied with the hares; they do not age nor die, but, one old one said, one would sometimes be killed by their number, this one being chosen by a sort of lottery, and its body buried with great pomp and general misery, and that from the grave of this perished sprite would arise its selfsame form, which would put forth like a tree and bear on its branches many acorns, these being their embryos, and from the death of one would come many."

Modern Text:

The linguistic-string that follows was received and transcribed on a psychic recorder set up in an undisclosed location, described only as a wooded area in the vicinity of the town of Mohra, in Sweden, April 1971. The received material was preserved on wire and later this recording was processed by a specially-programmed translating computer at a former Soviet university and this is the English translation:

> a number of breathings over—together are sun-rising—in us sun-rising/great joy—in breath of wood/wood is there for great joy in what breathes—we wish exhaling—sound inhaling what is in us to do—to breathe—to behold—to bury—to plant—to make—to imbue—to make-simple—to bear—to discuss-with-hares—to wait—to come-and-go—to visit-houses—to bring—to stop—to quit—to make-stop—to frustrate-toads—to hex—to vanish—a number of breathings over in us—together are sun-risen—together are leaf-turning.

The Chaos Into Time.

For all its pulpish failings, "Herbert West—Reanimator" has a morbid verve and humor that makes it rewarding reading. In one issue of *Crypt of Cthulhu*, Bob Price and a number of other authors wrote a round-robin sequel, "Herbert West—Reincarnated", was assembled involving Bob Price, Rod Heather, Brian McNaughton, C. J. Henderson, Joe Pulver, and yours truly. I took dibs on the final chapter, and endeavored to write something unsequellable. Finally, an excuse to write long chewy Lovecraftian sentences! I should point out that, prior to the events narrated here, Herbert West (after reanimating the remains of Jesus in a secret Nazi lab at Auschwitz— McNaughton's bit there) assisted the US government in reanimating the corpse of a the Roswell alien (Chris Henderson's idea—the alien wasn't riding in a saucer, it was flying freely along in the ether when it collided with the fabled weather balloon). This alien will play a role in the denouement of Herbert West's story.

The Chaos Into Time

I know my eyes are open. My eyes are surely open now. Wherever I sit, though I may only be a head on a table, it was forever my task to sit and tell, what West had shown me. Again and again, through death and death, I chronicled our experiments. I chronicled those experiments of which I was the innocent subject.

There is no soul left in me. My pseudonyms dropped away one after another, the plainest names, the most innocent and drab names, and now I have no name. Don't look past these lines, or in between—or look as you wish, drink your fill of nothing. I am less than a voice—this body of mine is a prosthetic limb, and the ghost pain for the original, pure, unviolated, (you'll excuse my laughter, if you can hear it) body of my innocence is long numbed and the nerves dead. My dead nerves tell me to tell you the last fable of our master Herbert West.

Mirthless laughter is an involuntary matter, excuse my tittering if indeed it is audible … and Herbert West was ever my rapist, he was my bride, my child, he made his latest debut parting the curtains of my own flesh and taking their substance, my master, my devourer, who leadeth me through the valley of the shadow, the substance, the unrelenting scourge of death the stench and the million lacerations of death and steeped me and scalded me in death, gave me death and birthed death in me—his needle and his serum deprive me of all comfort, he laid me down in a reeking grave and made a world of it for me, his will shall be done, yes in heaven too. He has baptized me in the earth, put me in my grave and brought me out, though from that moment on I am a child of the charnel kingdom of Death, and I walked in the lackluster sunlight with a grey heart choked with ashes, a withered brain like an aged leech in the dry pit of my skull, a body stretched on the wrack of a blasphemous parody of life without vitality. My endless life is only an expression of my slavery, a salt of shame to massage into my parched and bloodless wounds—but West's, his life could only be the tool of a will so monstrous, so towering, that it could brook no humanity, no contingency, no obstacle. West's will was a black lighthouse, a darkhouse, flaring its beams of life-sapping luster across the threshold of death, into the leaden, still seas of irretrievable silence and peace, and dragging therefrom, in violation of all that is natural, the mutilated remains, shivering and outraged, cast into the blazing crucible of West's insane will to be infamously transmuted by his supraSatanic alchemy into the living forms of the diseased abortions of his spirit. West admitted no limit, spared nothing. In the infernal economy of his experiments, nothing could go to waste, for West and Hell both feed on their own excrements. And, to West's eyes, everything was excrementa, material, mere matter to be assaulted, helpless and bleeding beneath the hammer of his impossibly inexhaustible fund of will.

What I did? What is there to tell? Herbert West used me again, of course, he tore himself from me, he used my very flesh again. We escaped that hospital, that poor fool sent to ease my mind (excuse my laughter again), and then I neither know nor care what transpired. I went with him, he pulled me, I went. I was with him, as the landscape changed all around us, I was with him, and then I was not with him. I remained where I was. There may be some reason to think that I remained there a long time. I have no particular impressions. I know there were no people with me, that there was nothing around me, that the sun came and went in the sky, and I seem to remember lying on the ground, watching the tree that raised its branches over my head growing. I saw its limbs stretch and grow, with no interest, a budding new mortality, only.

When I rose, and for what reason I have no answer, I had to pull myself out of the ground. What is there to say about what I saw—streets and buildings, sooner or later. I wandered the streets of that city, and sat by the side of the road. People would toss change at the ground around me, and I would sit and look at it, I would rise and leave it behind. My appearance in the cold and polished glass of the storefronts caused me no shock. I have always looked the same.

I knew what to expect, and I was not wrong to expect it. I suddenly felt my pace grow brisk along the street, I walked purposefully, with my eyes fixed forward, all the intensity of my gaze directed ahead of me, because I did not need to look to know that West walked with me. His blue eyes were hooded and he wore a strange smile, and without words he directed me to follow him. A plain house, as I expected, cool inside and lightly salted with a stench in the shadowy air, a basement door swung wide. Had I the merest shred of humanity left, had I been a person at all, I would have felt a clawing terror at the prospect of descending into that black basement, the slobbering demonic maw of a familiar Hell whose clutches I had eluded only for a moment.

"How fortuitous to have found you again," he said. "But then, I have always been lucky." He moved around the depths of his fathomless basement, turning on one light after another, none of them adequate, so that there grew up around him a feeble constellation of leprous, flickering bulbs, that shone on the grisly relicts so devastatingly familiar to me, and revealed, too, clusters of half-imaginary objects, shocking detritus whose uncanny contours were so abysmally suggestive, weirdly familiar machines of lewd designing, the obscene pudenda of a cancerous lich proffered from out of putrescent dimensions where the very darkness itself stank with rot.

"Recognized these, have you?" West glittered at me from the other side of a long table littered with these machines, and I did know them.

"They seem very much like the weapon of that star beast," my voice was a perforated tissue of corroded sound.

"I touched its mind!" West said triumphantly, still only a vague form behind the table. The time that had passed since then had done little to dampen his bottomless enthusiasm. "I learned its secrets—in a haze, like a child almost, I glimpsed such cosmic principles in that ancient mind, and since then I have been hard at work! I assure you, the weapon you mention was a plaything—a tool, if such a word may be applied to it, as elementary to that beast as a toothpick is to you. What I have seen blazing in that mind is the crystal lens of universal form, of the synthesis of dimensions … and my discovery, my newest works, are my greatest yet, though not the greatest to come …"

West had come around the table to my side: the expression on his face was the foulest possible distillation of gloating demonism, of an unholy avidity crawling in the wallows to the egress of an infernal intestine. He now gestured to a wall nearby. I blinked at the darkness, and he turned one of the battered desk-lamps on the table toward the wall—there I saw a teetering set of shelves, a salvaged sideboard with scarred cupboards and black shelves listing against the wall, and on those shelves, tucked into those cupboards, each with its own bleakly jovial name-tag, were human brains in seething jars, bristling with cruel electrodes and simmering in the reagent.

West made a theatrical sweep of his hand, "I've had the best minds at work on the problem."

With the rustle of a death-rattle in my constricted throat I read the names of prominent physicists, lionized specialists, cosmologists of the first water, some who were not even reported dead, hanging before the swollen congeries of tortured, blistering neurons in those jars. Morbidly overstimulated by electricity and mammoth doses of reagent, kept awake and staring and remorselessly agitated, I seemed to hear their agony through the glass.

"They have made possible the greatest economy of time," he said with a peculiar intonation. "Their assistance, though not indispensable, has accelerated matters considerably; even taking into account the necessity of replacing a few of the still-living originals with doubles of my design … Now, what do you make of this?"

West showed me a barrel-shaped assemblage of some greenish metal, that gave off a mildly acidic odor. I noticed, too, a transparent cylinder partially housed in the barrel, emerging from its nether side, and glowing with the phosphorescent gas it contained, which, by its color, could only be vaporized—and apparently highly volatilized—reagent.

I am sure I stared with utter vapidity, but West reacted as if I had evinced great curiosity.

"Observe!" he said, operating a small remote control, made of oddly filigreed metal.

There was a brief whine, which accompanied the appearance of a long and very fine needle from the front of the barrel.

"Mystified?" West asked with dismal glee.

"Of course," was my reply. Flat as was my affect, I felt a long unfamiliar fluttering of dread.

"Allow me to show you … the other half of this puzzle!" This other half was another device, a nauseous green metal case large enough to hold a man, and into whose "nose," for want of a better word, the barrel assembly he had shown me earlier was fitted, its needle flickering dangerously, pointing out the front like the nose-cone of a V2 rocket. The Stygian darkness within the case's compartment seemed to suck coldly on the air, and I glimpsed inside a glistening web of mucilaginous threads and membranes whose arrangement so offended by eyes and smarted on my brain that I recoiled involuntarily, much to West's amusement.

"You mere little man, do you know what this is? I won't toy with you—it is what simple minds would call a time machine."

I was brought up short—not so much by West's claim, which I did not doubt for a moment, but by the thought of the reagent gas in the barrel, and the long and incredibly fine needle whose point seemed to taper to infinity.

"… Perhaps all those years with you were not entirely wasted—if in fact you begin to grasp my purpose…" West mused.

"I am not sure …" then, as my faltering intelligence groped in squamous oblivion toward a conclusion, a realization barely without the reach of my grasp, I battered or blundered through the crazy-quilt of my deranged thoughts and emerged with a question, whose implications and whose answer I anticipated without clarity—but again and again the words shouted within the maggot-scoured hollows of my temples and chattered from my ruined mouth—

"… but why, why all this, why everything, West? Your mission—your goal, to cheat death? What was your goal, West?"

His eyes kindled coldly, but his candid face bore an unusual look, unusual even for him, as he gazed eagerly back at me.

"My goal? My why? I will tell you—did I hate death, and look upon it as an enemy? Yes! And why? Because death is the same, it is ignominiously the same, inevitable, and regular. I saw, from the very first, that life is chaos, that it is the free and ruthless experimentation of nature itself, but just when its most arresting, its most interesting, prodigies emerge into the light of the microscope and the vivisector's blade, up again bounds that hateful limit of death! Do you believe that I was seriously troubled by the failure of our first experiments, the mad beasts that rose from our tables, that had been the peaceful corpses of once-rational men?! Those were no failures! It was my intention all along to sow chaos, to uproot the regular and orderly progress of this unimaginative and simplistic life, to redress the insult of life's plainness, its tedious balances, its boring frankness and predictability! To deprive it of death's limit, so that life may not merely expand or diversify, but turn freak, turn mad, turn riot in flesh! ... But this world, this universe, is unworthy of madness, even reasoned madness! I have studied the structure of the cosmos, mastered the eldritch wisdom of our colleague from the stars whose tissues animate this capsule—and found that even it, the very universe, cycles through the blind turmoils of life and death, bursting into its full-dimensioned infinity, only to dwindle down to a single subatomic point again, a dead cosmic egg, awaiting the inevitable, natural revitalization. And what was my reagent, if not the ecstatic eruption of wild, rapacious energies alien to both life and death—a wild ferocity, a telluric force to shake the pediments of the heavens, pure chaos!"

Then I briefly, passingly, caught sight of the basis of West's limitless will, which had overwhelmed all in its path, like a patient conflagration; the white-hot hate that burned in West, an eternal, godlike hate.

"I have mocked," West ranted, his voice building to crescendo, "the empty miracle of birth, I have trampled death, conquered and razed death to the ground, I have wrestled with the cheap and slipshod biology whose curse you and the rest of mankind have so patiently and submissively borne, and I have bested it, shamed it, degraded it, time and again!

"... and that still wasn't enough ..." his tone dropped to a murmur, the rage slid off his face, and he grew calm, and a little grin that shook even me, was there on his clammy, foaming lips.

"... that still wasn't enough ... I had won—but only the battles. I had bested this nemesis time and again, but I was the victor only of skirmishes. The war raged on, on and on, as smug and complacent in its false security as could be—"

"West—what is the time machine for?" I blurted, in numb shock.

West gave me an indulgent smile, guessing my thought. "Do you honestly think I would be satisfied with that, with the mere undoing of life on this solitary planet? I have touched in dreams the elder genesis of aeons past—how should I trouble myself about this or that piece of slime on this or that primordial shore, when I could have it all?

"I brought you here ... how should I say, certainly not to share my triumph, but to witness it, as you have witnessed so many of the steps that brought me to this moment, and—to release you! To release you! Shall I grant your fondest wish? I set you free—from this day, from this very room, I shall vanish from your life, from life, forever, altogether! Paltry life, paltry room! I shall ride with the viewless wings of madness, of a madness on the level of matter itself! My reagent brings the dead back infected with the madness of that chaos greater than mere life and death, and into the hands of that madness I shall consign myself, its master, its God! The purest, the vastest, the supreme of all possible Gods, in a universe of my own making, and in my own image! And when I am gone, shall you come or go, stand there forever in your cosmic nullity? To your own devices then, and the vacuous, narrow existence you've selected for yourself—you never were up to the challenge, and were it possible for one of my stature to pity such a mite as you, I would."

He stepped into the time machine—which I now understood was oriented toward the future, and not the past, as I had thought at first. The hatch swung shut on its shrieking pneumatic hinges, swallowing for the last time, in any universe we know, the face of Herbert West—but his voice came shadowed out to me through the closing aperture in the side of the metal device, with its mysterious barrel-shaped assembly, a proboscis with a needle dwindling down to a subatomic point, designed—as I saw in a rush of revelation that battered to pieces the flimsy tissue of my mind—to piece a subatomic, cosmic egg—attached to a reservoir of plasmified reagent, that universal solvent of all sanities—his voice, which would shake a cosmos, spoke, before he vanished forever—with a last supercilious grin no doubt, he said,

"I go to watch the Universe itself die ... and when it does, *I intend to re-animate it!*"

The Depredations of Mur.

In general, horror fiction tends toward one of two effects, either proper fear, or melancholy. Frightening stories leave the reader in a state of startled anxiety, at least for a moment or two, with the familiar side-effects (reluctance to enter dark rooms, fitful glances thrown over the shoulder). The melancholy stories on the other hand will have a depressing and demoralizing effect, if executed correctly (an irritating effect otherwise). So here is one of many depressing stories. I was trying here to feel out the sort of place that vaguely takes shape in the yearning to escape a failed life; failure in life suits you to a certain grim success in the other place.

The Depredations of Mur

Prologue

[empty sky, no stars, no planets, no horizon. A high round moon brilliant with its own light, to which no object is presented, however, there are sounds: whining floorboards, padding of feet on planks and flagstones, creak of restlessly occupied chairs and a voiceless remark from volutes of interrogative smoke]

Part I

The day came well into the days of my life when I failed finally—for all time a failure, for all reasons. Now I don't remember what sent me back out into the street in a daze, for the last time … as far back as I can remember, I had been everywhere received as a gifted child; I had been fussed over like a prodigy. I had gradually seen the outline of my future life develop before my eyes, welcoming, bland; it seemed to be taking care of itself. At some embarkation point in the future, I thought, possibly after I would have finished with school, I would step off into my future life; its hazy lines would gel crisply around me then, and I would be born again.

I embarked as I expected I would. I stepped off, and nothing was there to receive my step, and I fell. I resolved, as though it were only a matter of being serious and wanting things badly enough, and embarked again and again, failed and defeated I had to climb back. That gesture of stepping off was an incantation I made more and more urgently; every time I made it, I made it in the fear that I had no life waiting for me at all. I would fail, and see it proven again: no life for you.

Years passed. I haunted my life. My family maintained me, the negative abundance of disappointments that constituted me, after their fashion. My spectral father, who died when I was young—a writer of unusual children's books; my irritable, severe mother, of the unexplained comings and goings, with her pinched intensity; Walter, my stepfather, a bookbinder … frankly mystified and defeated by my mother; and my two young sisters. I would hide from them all so as not to have to give them my blessing, my latest failure, to be joined into my particolored patchwork fool's uniform of failures. My mother greeted me on my every despondently brave return with grim satisfaction, but she never lectured; my stepfather's interviews with me were too mild and gentle to be called lectures, he only expressed sympathy and shared in my disbelieving and gradual resignation, asked me to try again …

and now and then, a suggestion, like a knife of goodwill.

I would lie on the floor of empty rooms here and there and keep as still as possible, because I had a propensity to scream at these times, and the urge to scream would come and go. Fractures run through the world, through me—I always rushed from failure to failure; as long as I did so, my forward momentum would hold the fractured pieces together—but, when I was unable to maintain that momentum between failures, the fractures would gape, and the pieces would begin to spread apart, like breaking ice floes, over nothing—once started there was no stopping the torturing spreading of the pieces—over nothing. They yawned apart opening terrifying gaps that would mean insanity to fall into the gaps, living death of sense—I had the terrifying and bizarre idea that, falling down there, I would not find myself *alone*. I had a propensity to scream, that would build in me when I felt this way—like running exhausted beyond endurance on breaking-up ice floes—I sometimes tried actually to hold my head together with my hands, as if I thought it would separate, and then I would scream a little into my sleeve or I would use my arm as a gag and scream into it.

*

[*rustle of fog on lead roofs ... on stone wands and buttresses in frigid sky ... through the conical roofs comes the sound of metal chimes dribbling on stone pavements ...*]

*

Someone must have taken some notice of me, though it took a long time. I was hiding. I had had one of these fits of muffled screaming, and when I woke up, I found a note lying on the floor beside me. Someone had quietly slipped it beneath the closed door, a foot or two away. My name was looped in unusual handwriting on the outside of the folded sheet.

Having failed at everything, I received word that my presence was requested at Mur.

*

[*leaves from a history of Mur: "... in legend, the founders of Mur had retrieved, at the cost of their own lives, an occult mathematics ..."*]

*

The light turned white in the moments immediately after the sun went down, as I sat in accumulating dusk and I glazedly stared at the note, a miraculous, terrible thing. I saw the note get pale and within a few moments turn blue, and I noticed the sky, which was like a flat ceiling of very high clouds so uniformly joined that they were a seamless sheet whose color was mirrorlike, like a mirror without reflections. That blue glow came and went, and when the room was dark I suddenly stood up, and I left, for Mur.

Things die down suddenly at nightfall in that town. While the press of people on the narrow boulevards doesn't diminish but actually swells and overflows the pavement, silence falls on them as the sun sets. In that press I seemed to hear a low murmur, and there was the shadowy name "Mur" insinuated in my ear … hearsed allusions and funeral occasions … death oracles … and new bodies for old … And though I couldn't detect the source of them, these voices caused me to feel (with despair) a sort of hope—because this time, if I was wrong, I wouldn't have the strength, (I *hoped* I wouldn't have the strength), to recover and return home. The vicelike idea that I wouldn't have the courage to make this my last chance squeezed me without crushing me, just at the limit of my endurance.

*

[*"… in a circle they had with carving knives loosed the 'bubbling hippocrene' from each of their breasts and in their final ecstasies babbled and murmured through mouths clogged with their own gore the secrets that appeared in their minds as they died …"*]

*

The streets were wet so that the asphalt was black and invisible, and only the scattered reflections of the streetlights shone there, making the humped street, bookended between the empty sidewalks, look like a plank of densely starry sky, dazzling enough to obscure the street that rose above it. As I walked, reflections slid along the wet lengths of scattered twigs on the pavement, making streaks like shooting stars. Where the streetlights, which weren't tall, shone behind the trees, they made those dripping sticks gleam and appear to spiral like a cobweb of minute fractures … and beneath, were the glistening trunks. I had a dreamlike feeling then, as if it were all before me on a page. The only living thing, (I won't include myself), was a cat, dozing in the window of a florist's. The cat started a little when I came into what must have been her view. She was reacting to the same invisible stimuli that worked on me as we both dreamed the same dream—and we shared that realization, too, as we looked at each other. I was a character in *her* dream.

*

[*bells are tolling their sound against rigid and featureless panes of air—the creak of bell-ropes and pulleys does not reach to the stone pavings at the base of the towers*]

*

The street turned and turned and grew thinner as if it were getting tired; I was following an irregular grassy bank along a sluice of traffic. I kept my balance gripping the damp stone wall above the bank, beaten back by the force of the headlights, like a relentlessly staring assembly line of eyes running back and forth like scanning lines. Ashamed, I managed to run some distance along the top of the embankment on a narrow lip of solid ground bordering the wall, but I was still probed by flaring and dimming headlights, which forced me to run on top of the wall. From there, a moment later, I dove into the graveyard.

*

[*"... to this fate were consigned all but two of them; the first of whom, as his colleagues cut themselves open, drank a lethal dose of vitriolic ink ... then, with the toxin in his veins, he took a tattoo dictation, inking the second man's skin with glyphs of poison, making him a living (dying) record of the revelations of Mur ..."*]

*

I was near the one end of the cemetery, where the broad street splits against its corner into the two roads that formed its borders. I could see the stream of lights rushing along the other side of the cemetery across from me, a few standing crosses and obelisks intermittently silhouetted against it. I was nearly at one corner of a mammoth diamond. I ran for the center, toward a line of trees, through the graves, running until there was no light. I couldn't stand being seen—I knew what they saw. I had gashed my arm coming over the wall, there was some blood. (New bodies for old: when a limb is amputated a ghost limb is still palpable ... I knew my whole body was the ghost of my true body—which was not then possible to imagine).

*

[*"... from their submerged bones and glassy flesh, and stony earth softened by the bloodbath, the edifice of Mur emerged ... the venom-letters were embodied in the structure, and were read in dreams by those who came after ..."*]

*

I cannot account for that feeling—a different kind of life altogether—invisible … weak. Looking at the trees against the sky as denser dark against lighter dark, I had a premonition, not for the first time, of unfamiliar senses that should have been proper for me, screened off behind a thin meniscus. The barrier was transparent enough that I could almost see through those other eyes, or sense at least through those other organs, though my vision was distorted by the trembling screen that stood between me and them, or between those two halves of me. I would say I reached for them, the other senses, but I wouldn't have known how to do that reaching—I only yearned for them.

*

[*wind sighs from windows that open just below the unbroken ceiling of clouds—mist drops from the sills like breath*]

*

The bitter air calmed me. In what light came from the sky, the grass was blue and the sour-smelling stones and statues were white and lambent enough to cast soft shadows, and the acrid earth was black. From there I was aware of some other lights. A sentence from one of my father's books appeared in my head as though I had read it there, "It is perfectly natural for the spectral eyes of ghosts to gather in the branches of trees."

They gazed at me, and my gashed arm, with a diffuse glow flickering brighter, without throwing shadows or hurting my eyes; that moonlight glow was so diaphanous it didn't touch me, though if it became brilliant enough I would disappear into it.

"By all means," I said, and made a courtly gesture.

Their scrutiny fell on me; their awareness of me approached like a lantern that obscures with its light the one who carries it—I had a premonition, from the manner of those eyes. The graves were stirring underground though the surface was still, as if they were shouting and applauding the gash bleeding on my arm, or responding to the pain themselves, with a crescendo I could barely hear. My blood looked like black oil in that light, my arm throbbed painfully. There followed a murmur, like an audience settling.

I walked off the paths and from plot to plot. The stones I touched were hot and vibrated as if they were stuttering. I could see clearly, the air was perfectly clear. I heard an inchoate voice letting out syllables into the air and realized my lips were moving, my throat was humming against my collar—I was asking the way to Mur. As my own eyes swept the ground, I saw a translucent arm emerging from a grave, as if the occupant had rolled over on her side and thrust her arm out into the murky air. It lay on the ground, round and faintly luminous, with a bangle on its wrist, and its finger pointed. I noticed a number of other graves had sprouted arms whose fingers pointed in the same direction. An occasional left hand would be protruding straight up out of the grave, the hand bent back at the wrist and pointing. I saw transparent arms like candle flames point from out of the branches of trees. The lines along which the arms were pointing converged over a low hill, the way to Mur.

*

[*shadowy filaments float like cinders up the wet stone walls and dance atop the spires like candle flames—below the towers ... a dark colossus of stone blocks with no human shape ... the horizon shrinks around its foundations*]

*

I crossed over the hill and followed the train tracks that ran over the graves at the base of its far slope. There was no wind. I passed through a shallow bed of trees, and, as I walked, the cemetery petered out into desultory graves with damaged or illegible markers. There was a train station within a few hundred yards of the line of trees. I drifted into its soft lights—the ground was covered with tracks and I could hear the sounds of a railyard; to one side I could see a large dark car spinning soundlessly, round and round, on the turntable used for reversing engines.

Inside the station, which was not much larger than a small house, and low-ceilinged, I could see a few passengers waiting on benches, stiff and motionless. Then they moved, or were caused to move—a train was leaving. The conductor was hurrying passengers on board and could only tell me that there was no such stop and that the train that was loading there was the last of the night.

*

[*ocean of slate-colored hills—pale grass flutters and lies flat where the wind rolls up and down slopes—crashes and breaks like water against unyielding shadow stones*]

*

Around the train station a town had collected, whose streets led into gritty bronze neighborhoods, dank and metallic like the bowels of a rotting ship. I wandered there with a strong intuition of patience. In one street, I saw a light in the who's-there panel of a heavy wooden door—this was the only light I had seen in any of the buildings.

The bookstore was large and airy inside, its heavy, freestanding shelves arranged to form a broad-avenued maze. When I noticed that most of the titles were old and out of print, and all of them for children, I began idly looking for the books I'd read as a boy. I got a number of shocks from covers I'd forgotten. On one shelf there was a series of books, well over a dozen, whose covers made a sequence like frames of film: the framed image rushing up to a battleship on an ocean as grey and flat as slate, closing on its uppermost deck, and the young bearded captain fiercely staring standing at the railing, who then turned into a carrion seagull of such startling malignance that I nearly dropped the book. (New bodies for old).

One set of shelves contained another, a small ornate antique bookcase all covered in black lacquer and minute strands of pale blue small-petalled flowers, with three shelves and several sets of small glass doors. I opened one of the doors, which was surprisingly thick and sturdy, and removed a book at random. The cover was blank, faded absinthe green. I opened the book and stared at my father's name on the title page.

I remembered this book. He had written it when I was very small. Sometimes, as a child, I would come awake in the middle of the night, and my father would be reading it aloud to me in the darkened room, sitting in the armchair that stood facing the foot of my bed. Even in passing recollection, I could hear his soft, measured, calm voice. I had lost the copy he had given me. When I checked the rear endpapers I found that this was *my copy*. My name was printed on the rear endpapers in my father's distinctive handwriting, that looked like typewriting. I clapped the book shut in my hand and started walking briskly.

*

[atop the walls air sluices in the unworn pathways and precariously elevated stone catwalks ... sifts in through honeycombs and wasp's nests of precipitated stone that hang in low fronds like stalactites from the eaves and grows in mirror-image stalagmites from the roof-edges and balconies forming in numerous spots a broad-avenued maze]

*

I visited a street cowled by humped trees, through whose low-hanging fronds I could see luminous houses. The first pedestrian I had seen all night came up through these veils: I saw the glinting of the buttons on his jacket first, then the gleam of his hat's black visor, and then his phosphorescent white collar. When he was within a few feet of me, I recognized his conductor's uniform, and at the same moment he softly asked me if I was on my way to the station.

He came up to me and I nervously asked him if there was a train to Mur— unaccountably nervous, I felt the gaze of those houses as I spoke the name. I could barely make out what his reply, but he knew the name and mentioned a very low fare. I reached for the money in my pocket, possibly with the idea of buying a ticket from him that moment, and dropped my change.

"Oh—I'm sorry," I started trying to pick up the shining coins but I didn't seem fully to understand how; I plucked at them without accomplishing anything and was alarmed. "Well this was clumsy of me—it's a good thing they shine or else—I can never hold on to money—does the train leave soon?—I have some ill relatives—the fare is sure low—." The conductor was crouching beside me, his soft dark hands avidly flicked up the coins and he pressed them into my hand as he found them. "Oh thank you—you don't have to—can I buy a ticket from you now?" He answered that I could. "I'm sorry I've forgotten what was the price?" I had not forgotten, but I was confused and somehow alarmed by his calm, measured tone of voice. He told me again. "Oh yes I'm sorry"—I counted the money in the dark and handed it to him. I couldn't tell what he made of my panicky insincere explanations. "Where is the train?"

He pointed. We were only a few yards from the corner, and beyond that, I could see the tracks, the dimly-lit back end of the station. I saw two pale cars sitting on the tracks.

I thanked the shady spot where I assumed the conductor was still standing, and went to board. Inside, the cars were dark, and redolent of varnish. Pale panels of light, punched out and slightly green-tinted by the windows, were lying canted on the backs of the seats, like antimacassars. I sat with one of these diamonds in my lap, and all at once was so relieved and so freshly aware of how far I had run and how long ago everything else was, that I fell asleep.

I awoke a few hours later. The train had not moved.

*

["... *over the following centuries, posthumous disciples of that occult mathematics made prismatic armatures ... which passed through protracted birth-pangs of miscalculation and refinement in the aftermath of nightmarish mistakes ...*"]

*

We went a far distance, there were no stops. My ticket had been taken while

21

I slept. The lights in the car came on so gradually and remained so dim that I wasn't conscious of them until later, when my own reflection dimly superimposed itself on the blur outside. Buildings all fell away. The train was nearly silent, and empty. I was able to go over in my mind my reasons for leaving; when I rubbed my numb eyes and cheeks my hand came away wet. The windows wouldn't open; I opened the door between cars and stepped outside into roaring night and the explosive clatter of the wheels.

Low tree-lined hills, perfectly dark, mounded up to one side, and salt flats yawned on the other. Overhead, the clear sky and constellations. There was a gust of wind that sucked me off my feet—if I hadn't seized the railing I would have been borne off into the sky. In the moment, when I was held at arm's length off my feet, apart from the shudder excited in me by my sudden lunge for the railing, I was not alarmed. I would have been glad if I hadn't been so agitated; I wondered if I should release my grip. The wind set me back on my feet.

Between the cars, a bubble in the middle of the wind, I wondered if, like a bubble, I might disappear if I touched any physical thing. There was no cowling, and both cars extended spacious tongues toward each other; the arch of open air through which I could see the black on black land and the sky was wide enough to permit me to fly out lengthwise should some force throw me off my feet. I cowered a little against the force of the wind; its touch was keen, as if my face and hands had been moistened. The train was flying on the rails, so fast it barely touched them, and with each gust of wind it bobbed slightly, so perhaps *it* wasn't held so tightly in gravity, either. I felt my eyes shining, my hands shook violently on the railings, I wanted to thrust my face into the slipstream sliding along the flanks of the car ahead of me.

I contented myself with the wind and view and soon felt renewed calm. I had not tried the door to the next car, where the conductor and driver presumably were. I could see a dim light in the window, through a drab curtain. I imagined something like a scriptorium or a sewing circle behind the door, many people, huddled and silent, doing intricate, eye-consuming work—but as I pictured this my curiosity weirdly drained away, my legs began to hurt, and I went back to my seat in the second car.

*

[*"... but these initial errors were not the worst ... the most damning results ... were the consequences of the final perfection of their machines ..."*]

*

Waking up from that sleep was a protracted business, like trying one key

22

after another in a door. I came awake surrounded by trees ... the rails curved in a generous ellipse away from me, and the train was just passing from view.

I had been deposited in the branches of a tree, which gave way when I tried to get up, sending me crashing through the bracken. I came to rest at the base of a bank, a little above the edge of a river. Its surface was crêpey, its flow sluggish, its breath clammy and a little fetid, all black as a flow of bronze. I remember standing on the bank watching it with a familiar premonition of patience.

Out of the trees on the opposite bank, came the note of a dull sullen bell, in slow tolling, dropping the leaden knell of its tone like a pall in layers on the river, over the trees, ringing down on me its doleful pulse—the knell of Mur.

*

[*"... those of their number not involved with the experiment merely died ... or lost their minds ..."*]

*

The current swept me off my feet at once—I was carried downstream, but managed to claw my way to the opposite bank after what seemed like a very long time, ending up jumbled in hard roots. Through these trees, their branches and their roots, both above and below ground, I easily followed a path of funereal clay, slick, pallid, and convoluted as an intestine. Hampered by drenched clothes and on flopping shoes, all the same I was racing, as if the path had a current to carry me. The path became overgrown and disappeared in boulders. I crawled through titan roots. Then the land opened out blue rolling waves and black crags, girdled in spidery copses, mountainous bands of crocodile teeth and upright saw blades of stone. It was still night, I turned this way and that to get my bearings, but I only caught sight of the edifice when I turned very sharply and suddenly.

Part II

[*"... the aim of these experiments was unguarded ...they would study what could be seen through their lenses ... and the faces of long-dead divinities ..."*]

*

The night had taken on a different quality. I made my way through the big black blocks that were scattered in the high grass about the foundations. There was a meager blue light that seemed blown to and fro on the wind like pollen, and which came from somewhere above the pitchy clouds that, despite the wind, from horizon to horizon hung motionless. The extreme cold was exhilarating, lightening my head.

I forget what the inscription or sign may have looked like—perhaps there was no sign, and I simply said "Mur" to myself. I do remember the completely unfamiliar, luxurious sensation that came over me as the gloom of the portico, deep and narrow, embraced me, and the cavernous chambers opened to greet me with their dank, sour breath. I picked my way through patches of rubble, in and out of unstable rents in the walls, until I found a small room, scarcely more than a closet—a stone closet, a mausoleum set in the wall—with a fluorescent window whose surface showed only inky darkness. I made myself comfortable there, carefully sealing myself behind its door.

*

[*the sound of a door softly striking its jam, the click of the latch, carries from hall to hall*]

*

I had turned and seen the terrible silhouette, mauling the sky with static violence. The bloom of its shape crept across my eye ... it sank its ghostly roots down in my breast. Under that outline I will always be.

I once had to escape somewhere ... now Somewhere is where I am.

*

[*"... dimensionological researches, in which the spatial and temporal extensions of physical objects were extracted and preserved ... grids of shimmering silver threads, dripping with frigid water, drawn from collapsing vanishing things ..."*]

*

Let me think again, and reflect on my first days there. There was so little light there. Night and day alternated only in the barely-noticeable fluctuations of the amount of light that haunted the crevassed, dusky undersides of a static roof of thunderheads. I saw no one, and there was no evidence of anyone—I never had the sense of being anything but alone, although from time to time it may have seemed otherwise. But I had no reason to assume that these other figures I would occasionally glimpse were not me. I saw no reason to assume that each part of Mur might not have its own time, and that I might not see from one time into another, depending on my position in the structure.

I could not account for my invitation ... or for the tolling of the bell.

*

[*"... but none who were there remained when they first looked out of the world ..."*]

*

("So I came to that place of reeking jewels, mold and gold, baroque slime and grave bile, that defunct monastery palace of cenobitic recluses, which is Mur, which is half a speech, a dusky syllable dropped into an echoing gulf and returning, having met and coupled with its double, as a murmur ... a haunt of death and ravenous undeath, of rats beetles snakes fungous flies worms dust cobwebs and spiders moths bats and all manner of living carrion like myself ... a composite cenotaph whose every oozing stone is ornamented with the memory of a chiming suicide, a crumbling through infinite layers of abjection.")

Barely a few days after my arrival, it dawned on me, and I remember at this moment a bracing but not strong breeze ruffled over me through a tattered aperture in the immensely thick walls—amazing realization: *I was perfectly suited to Mur.* The qualities that had made me an unsurpassed failure in the world were precisely the qualities that made me *perfectly suited to Mur...*

*

[*"... resort was made to an unbroken trance ... to forestall catastrophes like the one that claimed that generation of disciples lost upon the perfection of their armature ..."*]

*

I sustained myself foraging in the litter of overrun floors, where copious, greasy vines had widened the windows of some of the lower apartments, and some edible plants grew in the leaf-mold. There were a handful of gardens higher up in the structure, and some of the basements were partially flooded—there were fish in the brackish water, not hard to catch, although I found they came apart if seized too roughly.

... in finding a simple way to live I could not fail to realize that I would certainly die in Mur, alone, helpless and in silence. And I thought, by all means let my flesh rot and slough off, let me be a stained tea-colored skeleton, so that out of my false face might bloom the skull's imperishable grin ... my

25

true face ...

*

[*"... a state of permanent hypnosis ... a mesmeric trance enduring unbroken throughout the remaining life of the subject, who thereby becomes a mirror in which what is Gorgon-like can safely be seen ..."*]

*

I searched those chambers, so like a skull's, with a lamp in my hand, through carcass gardens fenced in battered ruins and rain-filled urns with lids of congealed scum—wading through brittle waist-high grass that rattled in the wind, my lamp sending angular shadows to flicker behind the colorless stalks that parted over ponderous armorial engravings and coarse carvings of beasts in weeping stone.

Daily, I accumulated more spaces for my collection, casting my nets and gathering in butterflies of empty space from the communicating vessels and stone webs of Mur's invisible architecture. I would be carried through Mur, a museum of rooms, a zoo for the insensible life of rooms—or for the life of what decomposes the life of rooms. And at times a weird joy, a morbid overexcitement, would froth up in me and I would rush along with my head in shadow like a dark lamp, wanting to gorge myself on Mur's mysteriousness because I wanted to feel too much of it and disappear, learn to breathe anguish like oxygen, nourish my ghost on Mur's air petrified in the corridors lying flat in the small rooms hanging like dampening tapestries in the vast rooms ...

... to fly on my feet and suddenly vanish, leaving behind a little crash of silence to fall back in a recumbent wave on the unbroken silence, that had endured there ... the untriggered echo of that crash would slide across the surface of the older silence, and go on gathering strength from the ever-growing distance of its eternal retreat.

*

[*"... the heart of Mur ... a prismatic hole, hemmed round by a party of incurable somnambulists ... never emerging from their séance ... peering at the cadaverous forms of deities that bob in dark intramundane sluices ... and somehow translating this phantasmogorical intelligence of theirs to what others there were ..."*]

*

After scrambling through racketing attics, I found I could get no higher in the structure than one of the clock towers. The face had fallen in and lay flat on its crushed works; its raised outer edge had allowed water to collect—the face had become a weed-choked pool, though not a stagnant one—the arms of the clock still swept across the dial and stirred the sluggish water, setting in motion a current in which the long green tresses of the weeds undulated clockwise.

I engorged myself with the view from the vast aperture left by the clock-face, though it was bearded with moss that hung down like seaweed and streamed in the wind.

I would return, though not in the "evening," with my lamp, through a forested attic rustling with invisible birds.

*

[*"... of that ultimate trance ... there was no power that could erase the markings left on their minds in the course of their aeons-old trances ... not that could erase them so well as to leave* absolutely no *trace ..."*]

*

When I lay on the floor to sleep, sometimes pacing my dark room beforehand, I would see, through the hazy marks flared into my eyes by the gleams of my phosphorescent window, what appeared to be a particulate cloud of greater darkness seeping in under my door. That door was as black as a chasm, and with increasingly violent thrills I would sense or imagine the presence of something inhuman roving Mur with terrifying speed from room to room, rushing up to my door, which would shudder explosively as it hurled itself against it ... there would suddenly burst on the silence a rush of heavy footsteps thundering to my threshold and the door would suddenly bang back on its hinges and through it a huge flailing shadow...

*

[*"... to expose their waking minds to the merest trace of what they had seen in their trances would have been enough to occasion shocking transformations ..."*]

*

Nervously, I listened to the silence there. There was nothing to hear—but what is the use of "there was nothing to hear"...

Squeezing myself into the corner of my room, not blind, but seeing nothing a black chasm, not deaf, but hearing nothing a soundless roaring. What I could see there, what my looking would find … absolutely nothing—but I shook uncontrollably imagining the sound that might brush against my ear, that silence had another side perhaps that was palpated by ghostly fingers—I would go insane if I heard a voice … the dark around me already seemed to be quaking with the screams I felt stirring buried down in my chest … coming right up to me, nestling beside me, gluing my ear, my helpless body falls apart—the voice is warm, soft, insinuating … or what begins as a phantom in the ear or imagination becomes more and more clear, welling up plain like a slow-rising bubble, a *thin* voice … a *thin* far-off wail … a fractured voice, faint, reedy … an icy drop in my ear … that the nothing might *address me* …

*

[*"… those whose gaze finds the dead world from which all life and motion come will be claimed by it … and drawn into its obscurity. Changed and claimed by that dead world, the medium can transmit only his own phantom death-throes … in chaos that palpitates in his own body … and through all matter and all bodies nearby to him …"*]

*

I remained quiet in the walls and listened without knowing when the gaze of Mur, which surrounds its structure like an intangible column bracing the rafters of the clouds against its deep-plumbed foundations, would suddenly notice me, and concentrate all its weight on me. I turned my father's book over and over in my hands looking for something, as if there were another way of opening it. I would sit for hours perfectly still, rigid in a chair, looking at nothing, wanting to be frozen like a statue when Mur would turn its gaze on me.

I knew something was happening. Completely alone, I should have become anything I wanted to be, everything particular about me would become elective. In time, I should have lost my name, my language, and become nothing, insane. Something that did not have the right was causing me not to lose my shape.

*

[*"… in the final trance however, the medium's suspense is perfect; he may see without being claimed by what he sees, and translate what in transmission would be madness, on the level of matter … around its mediums, disciples drew the figure of the unseen cosmos at a glacier's pace … advancing as inexorably, with a glacier's inhuman patience …"*]

*

In the portrait gallery, the paintings that hung on the wall showed only vacant rooms. I examined many of them closely, looking for any trace of an invisible figure—they were *portraits*, bearing small plaques with names barely engraved on them. But I saw only room after room. Most seemed to be rooms of Mur; some I recognized, others looked out over an unfamiliar ocean that lay like a band of lead against the horizon, and there were views of featureless landscapes showing not so much as a stone or blade of grass. As in dreams, the sun was never to be seen in those skies. All these rooms had visible doors, and these doors were always open, such that every portrait was a window on a deep or shallow abyss. Maybe these evacuated spaces were the proper objects of the portraits. I felt a sudden inundation of horror when I came to the last, which was a portrait of the portrait gallery, hanging like a mirror on the wall, a mirror from which I was absent ... behind me, in front of me, the door gaped—there a dim plummeting hallway, and the suggestion of a murky silhouette of glowing mist ... I ran down the gallery...

*

[*the sound of footsteps, echoing without dying*]

*

I was only playing. My running from room to room was a misuse of Mur, most likely, though I don't doubt a common one. I disrupted Mur with my own business, reading alone and in silence in the hollow middle of that cyclopean structure booming with lightlessness.

I would walk in Mur, and though I was passive and wandered here and there just looking at everything, all the same, my eyes were passing over the spaces of Mur as they would scan a written page. Haphazardly, knowing or unknowing, I took in the terms of the lineaments of Mur's structure, planted without depth, in mesmeric characters that had been shone into the stone. What I learned appeared in my mind, came to my notice, as a certainty, that I was playing, that what patiently waited to be revealed to me, after that playing was through, would weigh on me, heaviest of all, not the end, not my end ... but to be consigned, like Mur itself, to mere existence, forever.

*

[*"... the venom-letters were embodied in the structure, and were read in dreams by those who came after ... "*]

*

In the library, which was also a scriptorium, the shelves lined with mildewed books passed from sight into lightless zones further back in the walls. From between a pair of little carvings—apelike men with their heads thrown back, round eyes bulging, their wide mouths hanging open in cretinous grins—I extracted a hodgepodge volume that might have been called "A Book of Mur" or "A History of Mur." I read it perched on one of the high copyist's chairs, by a blasted window fringed with broken glass—through that, a sky that never moved. The high, stork-like desk upon which I leaned this book was all of shining wood, whose ebon varnish was criss-crossed with illegible scratches. Beneath this volume ... I found my father's book lying open to the rear endpaper.

In motionless hours I read my father's book. As I read, I played a game with the words. I flipped the pages and selected the first, or sometimes the second letter on each page. These formed the interrogative sentence:

"When is your father not yours?"

Like a machine I returned to the beginning and ran hard-eyed through the book a second time, selecting the letters, by what instinct I do not know, in a subtly different way. I had the feeling of playing a trick, of audacious deceptiveness. The second sentence was a variation on the first, and provided the answer to its question:

"When he is *ours*."

*

[*silence—wherever in the walls you are*]

*

I was with my father, whose name was also mine, when he died. We were crossing a public square—my father stopped to look up at the moon, which very suddenly had appeared nearly overhead. I looked at him: his attention was completely concentrated on the moon, and there was a communication there between them—his hand fluttered up to brush lightly his chest, where he lightly brushed the spot over his heart with his palm and the tips of his fingers. At that age I was exactly level with the hand he held to his chest. From where I stood very close to him, I remember his being even more infinitely massive than other adults, and shadowy and obscure in plain sight, more like a part of the landscape than a man, and more and more so just then. He tapped my arm. He said, "I have something to tell you ... you must remember M ... U ... R, **MUR**."

Before I could speak ... what life there was in him dropped below the level of his head ... this betrayed by the flicker I detected around his eyes as they drained ... and he leaned to one side with his all at once uncanny face still upturned, and collapsed dead to the ground, falling in a rigid way, already a thing.

My mother retrieved me and compelled me to repeat this story many times. Without a moment's evidence of surprise, she questioned me closely many times about the expression on my father's face, about the appearance of the moon and the various signs of communication that I noticed. That my father was now looking back at us from the moon, was not in doubt. My father's face had been like the moon, in that a shadow would pass over its features periodically. He had always been pale, and when he read to me in the dark, his face and hands glowed with a soft blue flame. After my father's death, I sometimes saw this same shadow—all shadows are the same—pass over my own features, and saw in the dark the same weak light playing around me.

My mother considered this my inheritance. From that moment, she withdrew from me *decisively*, and with a certain *satisfaction*.

From that time, I waited. For the most part, without knowing I waited. My waiting proved catastrophic for me; it caused me entirely to lose my track, and in that way I lost the world piecemeal. When the time came for me to go out on my own, I had made myself useless by this waiting. I was of no use to anyone or to myself. I was a high-strung fool in a pathologically vulgar melodrama.

From a window I noticed, across the shaft, a few levels below me, in a high-elevated, protruding cloister, some person, who was kneeling slowly down beside a lit taper in a candlestick ... wearing a robe or a skirt that slid along the ground unevenly at the kneeler's feet and swelled as he or she dropped. I saw that skirt put out tendrils and feelers, and, leaning forward, I saw there was no skirt but a dark pool spreading out in a wide circle around this person who leaned on horribly white hands and bled ... shrinking, feeble, waves of fatigue that I could feel from where I stood, a vertigo of blood sluicing from the body running out from quaking muscles sighing out from emptying tissues, and as the figure fell forward it raised its head, the candle, whose oddly bright white flame was the only light, toppled with a brush of one of those hands, and of the face I saw only a nightmare white brow write its streak in the blot of shadow that engulfed it. Then I didn't see it any more. That was me, dying.

*

[*volutes of interrogative smoke drift rise slow, and drift to a halt with a click*]

31

*

I had thought I was going to ornament Mur with my death. What others there might have been passed in review, could be parsed in the long individual lines of an endlessly extended stanza, its rhyme scheme increasingly distorted.

There were deep wells sunk into the structure, like the hollows of marrow bones adorned with arrogant spirals, flung aloft like carrion wings, whose plinths hung down in leprous plumage, altogether as bleakly ephemeral as the lacy long-veined traceries of dead sea foam green with asphaltum, but fitted so firmly that the worm-riddled wood barely complained under my weight. These titan staircases unfolding like the pinions of a jaundiced book, rattling its yellowing leaves, traced an infinite series of perforations, chiseled into the gneiss of the walls, in which reposed a god's ransom of reliquaries: around each grisly relic were mounded over heavy cowls of gold and silver and precious stones, weird ivories and feathers and the diverse plunder of beasts, ropes of swollen pearls purulating from platinum flames—to ascend those demented stairs was to follow a blazing delirium dragging into exhausting quadrilles of filigree and anguished detail, a tormented helix of embellished anatomy: a brown tooth pressed into a pink velvet pad beneath a flawless crystal lens; the jumbled phalanges, radius, and ulna, riveted in the sleeve of an upraised silver arm, the fingers, fixed in a gesture of blessing, caked with lurid gems; vials of powdery carmine blood, clotted against the crystal in brackish transparent webs like broken glass, all its scarlet heat banked down into dead embers, and webbed round in copper threads; and most wounding to the imagination, those imperishable skulls housed in portraiture-busts, the now fleshless faces glowing through false visages so wild, so ravingly overdone, as to disintegrate into myriad subdividing details torturously untraceable for the smarting eye. Tower upon tower this gargantuan collection might have memorialized every life ever lived, each corpse a livid coral studding reefs of stone, attended, for all I knew or could see, by spectral shoals of invisibly incandescent spirits—and when inclined I would imagine I could see the ghosts of the departed, crouching in each alcove, perhaps staring out at me, perhaps, and I can't explain why I should imagine this, awkwardly hanging out of their alcoves, plaintively brandishing their reliquaries, although not *at me.* I seemed to see those reliquaries petalled with ghastly white fingers, stalks of straining tendons, leaves of lilting shroud dappled with sunlight of bloody drops. There were none to see the reliquaries but me. Contemplating the mass of the remains it seemed all the same to me whether these dead were memorialized or not, their memorials no less lost to memory than were they. Not memorials at all—there were no names, no writing anywhere. For all I knew, it was a single body, perhaps a giant body, disarticulated and filed without notation in the charnel stacks of Mur.

These reliquaries were the immortal echoes of what Mur might remember, and still lived through long ropes of time into the present. They were like those vivid impressions that sometimes shock a memory nearly into view, but only in an outline that defeats recollection's ability to fill it. I looked to see if there were any there standing empty, waiting to receive my body, all tumbled in its parts—no sign. What dark-faced angelic messenger would be born out of *me* ... and close around my remains?

*

[*"... the mediums sustained their trances for aeons ... and spoke with glacial slowness until death would begin to overtake them ..."*]

*

Walking through the cloisters high above the ground reading my father's book, I find one of the illustrations that had terrified me as a child: it showed a lean man with black pits for eyes, descending a staircase from an open trapdoor, his features slit open in a black grin. When the page turned, there was a nearly identical picture, and the man's mouth hung open in his pale face—three black pits, with his eyes. They sucked at me. When I would look at him, my mind was clouded and the brightness of his face was so glinting that I blinked, and in the flicker of my eyelashes my father's features became recognizable on the page.

At night, I would wake up and find him reading aloud at the foot of my bed in the dark, lusterless eyes like two dark clouds smudging his drained white face. I read the text that accompanied the images. Some letters were unclear and went unnoticed by me except as blemishes that masked the story beneath, whose proper letters were clear: a counterfeit man, an imposter who was an entirely different man, only to be again unmasked as another man, and then another mask fell away to reveal another mask, which fell ...

And beneath so many masks, there might not be anything like a man. Who was it, to begin with? The black pits were its *original* eyes—what do black pit eyes see?

*

[*"... they would be the inheritance of a distant generation of disciples ... who would know the signs of dissolution and perform such tasks as would prepare the dying medium for the end of his trance ... and the realization, as the trance lifts, of what has been seen ..."*]

*

Somewhere in the place I could hear a disgusting liquid rustle—I imagined something like a huge caterpillar. Repellent, the sound drew me, and all at once I was groaning and crying.

I came to a landing above a collapsed staircase—over the banister the stairs broke off and hung ragged, and beneath, a slough of muck. There was something emaciated, like a skeleton, crawling down there—long threads of rancid black blood hung down like rent fabric all over its body, blackened slick and corrupt glistening like oil. It crept out from a spot beneath the landing in a thin mist of cold steam and turned, its head dangling and ribbons of tarry blood and thick fluid the color of sour milk hanging from its chin and drooping lips. As it moved in the muck its hands and knees made the gelatinous noise I had heard.

I looked at this thing, and it raised its head, shining up at me a terrible, *intelligent* look, from empty, vomiting sockets—frail ticking cadaver, blind … I could hear its *thin*, hoarse voice gasping.

It crawled a little further and then collapsed on its face—I was groaning and sobbing but my breath could not summon my voice, "p-poor, p-poor …"

*

[*"… and the transformation that follows …"*]

*

I did not know, until I turned to go, who I had seen—who it was *going to be*—who would in the portrait of the portrait gallery, appear in the long hallway …

*

[*"… by means of which the medium will cheat death …"*]

*

Visible all around me the words and sentences of Mur that burst out of the earth from dead bones and clotted blood come spiraling in around me like nets of mortuary earth paragraphs of headstones the hidden writings reading me, who trapped me on this page … who is trapped … who watched me … who reads me? I missed them—or we missed each other—just outside on the walls of Mur—hanging there like bats in windless air … biding by the

34

foundations in burrows—patiently waiting in the earth like toads ...

They crept after me ... on all sides they have gathered to listen ... a fresh idol for their pantheon, that was me for them ... the thread of my fate rasping in a straight line pulled through me, my head—I felt their tugs on that thread ... drawn into that circle one of many, many ... strange comfort in that thought and unwarranted, just let me not bear that title god alone but just as long as I'm one of many, many ... though dead but only present in a little divine space by merit of what I reflect back, of use to them, the gorgon-faced, pit-eyed fathers ... I reflect the talking masks of dead divinities because I am like them a *rotting spirit* ... all the time readying for my moment to embark ... I have not embarked once not yet ...

*

[*walls of upraised hands galleries of chants—the stones of Mur ring and ring round*]

*

Where was I?

I was lying on my face, where I had fallen, from the balcony above the staircase and the window there, dropped onto a sloping roof, lead panels—watching a uniform fall of rain chiseled from the clouds—I was soaking into the panels, the water riling around me, gluing me to the metal ... too badly injured to drag myself away, I expected to remain there until I dissolved and ran down into the silently-warbling gutters, where the corpse of a cat was mired in a clot of twigs and sludge, its head bobbing with the idle pulsations of the drains.

No ... Where was I?

I remained in the narrow room I had chosen. In the spacious halls of Mur moonlight was glowing, shining up from between the stone pavements ... a shape rushed from room to room looking for me ... I saw it when I shut my eyes and felt the shudder swelling in the floor ... for the first time I rose and opened my black window ... in the wind that followed, as the time went on, the things of Mur vanished one by one ... the bell tower ... the clock towers ... the attics ... then the walls, ceilings, and floors unlaced and faded, their contents dropped out of sight ... far below, when my window came open, there was a prismatic window ringed round in blackly shimmering figures ... Mur disappearing bit by bit reminded me to look through the window occasionally where the figures were still as they were around the lightless prism holding them, and venerated murmurings collected by the disciples who tended them, gaze averted, taking dictation ... from all around there was coming and going sliding through deepest depths, chaos of noise of collapses of   winds ... wild howling of the bell ... in my door where a dark figure with beautiful snowy hands took my hands, their hands cradling the pit gaze of Mur, two voices speaking quietly across the threshold of my room ... where the shock of a recognized voice grips the one living body, emanating screams and pulling on its hands that are held ... the hands held me ... touch as diaphanous and light as brushed by moonlight ... taken in hand to the window when it was a prism becoming deeper and deeper—visitations stirred in it ... on the floor of the heart of Mur where they were standing around it and moved aside to reveal it, in that heart every part of me gave way—the blazing moon hung in the sealed room staring down at me like a faceless face in the light of an overturned candle from whose plume of interrogative smoke a voice boomed—invisible flame hands reach for me ...

*

[*"... the disciples wait to see the change ... they see it ... and what they see is nothing human ... and what they see they venerate ..."*]

*

I am dreaming ... and I know that when I awake, and the dream ends, the one who dreamt will disappear—I will be transformed, and disappear ... and the dream itself urges me to wake. So I am going to let go the veil I am now too weak to hold. This is the end of my dream.

Dr. Bondi's Methods

The Moral Institute is situated in the nearly-abandoned city center, among the larger administrative office buildings of the Godavian capital. This area has none of the liveliness of the more outlying quarters, and so there is less to distract me from the general feeling of bristling, unfriendly observation that has haunted me since I passed customs. Auto traffic is almost entirely confined to the outskirts of town, which is girdled round with a moat of roaring, racing cars at all times, and banned beyond a certain point in the interior of the city. My cab lets me out at one of the concrete roadblocks, striped red and black, and I walk streets that grow wider and wider and emptier and emptier, and fewer and fewer. Soon they are only so many short, fat connecting passages between vast, staring squares. Each succeeding square gapes larger than the last. The day is shrilly clear; the sun blazes on ugly, overcomplicated fountains and stone buildings inexplicably ornamented with carvings of American Indians and Persian centaurs ... the squares are all paved with incredibly long, narrow stone slabs fitted together with barely-perceptible seams between them ... as I cross them, I feel like a mouse or a bug rushing over an empty hardwood floor. I see only the occasional figure now and then; some hurry out of sight, a few loiter in the shadows with their hands in their pockets, apparently nonchalant but still seeming to hide ... in this atmosphere of complete exposure to view, I don't blame them ... sheets from the *Godavian Observer* somersault lazily in indented gutters, or scud by me, hunched like crabs. Despite the brilliant sun that flares directly overhead, the wind from the mountains that ring the town freezes, buffets in random flurries from all directions, scrapes the squares antiseptically clean. I can't see any birds. A heavy, physically tangible silence drapes these squares.

Surrounded by empty museums with pinched little classical facades, and blank-faced office buildings, the Moral Institute is a colossal rectangular steel-and-glass block resting incongruously on massive, ancient-looking stone foundations. After walking for a long time I find the entrance at street level, a window-walled lobby like any modern bank's. Almost the moment I give my name I am whisked into an elevator and readily conducted into the presence of Dr. Nuoti Bondi himself. One of the persons surrounding him mutters something about "United States journalist" and Dr. Bondi emerges from the circle to give me his cordial, practiced, firm handshake. He is a medium-sized man with abundant curly dark hair and sparkling light eyes, sallow and pasty in complexion. As he draws near I find him faintly redolent of paraffin. He greets me in striking, luxuriant tones, and exhibits all the standardized social easiness of the continental smoothie, dismissing his associates after a few brief instructions, so as to give me—and in such a way as to make me feel that it is a privilege—his undivided attention.

Before we set out, however, he magnanimously agrees to give me a brief history of the Moral Institute. Some male nurses set up a card table and a couple of folding chairs in the corridor, and place before us a pair of cheese sandwiches wrapped in wax paper and two bottles of fruit juice.

I take note of his formal attire—it's the first icebreaker that occurs to me. "You look as though you've just come from church."

"I have," he glances at me as he leans forward, and then sits, "—it's a dreadful nuisance but attendance at the black mass is compulsory."

"Did I hear—*black mass?*"

"Oh the country's been Satanist for years—" he says, shaking his head in an offhanded way and yet as though to dismiss all doubt, "... it's not something that we advertise, so don't feel bad if you weren't aware of it."

I feel certain things falling into place. Nonplused I say the first thing that comes into my head—I realize, things are not going well—I can't seem to concentrate on what I'm saying. "That would make Godavia the first Satanist nation, to my knowledge."

"Well, you'd be surprised—but this brings us handily to the question of the Institute's foundation."

"I'm all ears." I recognize my state of mind; I've had these episodes before; for some reason, everything I say sounds facile, idiotic; but I can't allow that to distract me. I redirect all my attention in an exaggerated concentration on Dr. Bondi.

He pauses and purses his lips a moment in thought. "I'm going to have to approach this in a bit of a roundabout way, if you don't mind."

"As you think best."

"You have no doubt heard of the perennial battle between good and evil ... ?"

After a moment I realize he is waiting for an answer—"... If I'm not mistaken, it's the common theme among most religions."

"Yes that's it." Sharp intake of breath in the nostrils. "... Historically speaking, we here in Godavia are in rather unusual circumstances in that this allegorical struggle, for us, has taken on concrete reality ..."

"You mean to say there's been actual fighting?"

"Actual fighting, yes—underground Satanic cults flourished here in Godavia for generations, especially in the old pagan mountains. Their traditions are very old, untraceably old. What's more, our historians reckon that, owing to our remoteness, Godavia was something of a haven for persons fleeing accusations of witchcraft elsewhere. Well, not to go on and on about it, apart from minor flare-ups, things ran fairly smoothly in their courses until the Christian revival of the 1920's, when ... these fellows ... embarked on an ill-advised series of persecutions. While on our end we were not at all a unified church, we set aside our personal differences—momentarily—to defend the cause in general from what appeared to be a genuine threat of total extinction."

"You're describing a domestic religious war."

"Quite so, yes—we fought, and we won!" He says this with evident satisfaction and bites into his sandwich. I taste mine and find it a little stale. Sensing a lag coming on, and wishing to avoid it even at the cost of seeming dim, I ask: "But good and evil as such … are you suggesting the eternal struggle of good and evil has been resolved here?"

He purses his lips again and ponders with little nods. "Ehm, at least insofar as we can talk about institutionalized good and evil. While I am not able to speak to conditions obtaining elsewhere, I am able to say with confidence that *here* and *for us* the battle is most decidedly over."

"So, were all the Christians here exterminated, or driven out?"

"Not everyone no … there are other sins than sins of rage, for one thing. But most of them were killed … and the remainder are safely in hand."

"I can't manage to imagine it—did you have … armbands? and banners … ?"

"Heraldic devices are an important part of Godavian culture, always have been." He taps the golden crest on his signet ring.

"And all the Christians fought … ?"

"Ah, no, I see your meaning—some fought, but the vast majority were entirely passive. I suppose they were modeling themselves on Nero's victims— or Ghandi, perhaps. You might think of Ghandi … his challenge to the British was, in essence, that 'you will have to kill us all if you wish to keep hold of our India'—now suppose the British had taken them up on that!"

"I begin to see how this one-sided victory is possible, but—to extend your analogy—what is the profit to the English in owning an empty country?"

"An astute question … well they wouldn't have stood to profit much from owning the world's greatest cemetery—not right away, but in the short term they don't deny themselves the great pleasure of this massacre, and in time they might have populated the entire subcontinent themselves, in which case they would still have India today, wouldn't they?"

Dr. Bondi seems to read some doubt on my face, but he grows more animated. "The analogy is perhaps not so good … of course, the task is considerably easier fighting your own kind on your native soil. The Vikings never conquered much despite their extensive travels—and why is this? They could have ferociously battened down enduring footholds along the Atlantic coast and built themselves a far-flung empire big enough to rival Rome—and did they? No. Instead, they whittled away at themselves in miniature civil wars. Why? I contend they preferred intelligible victims—perhaps it was better fun killing people whose screams they could understand."

I suspect Dr. Bondi is changing the subject. I eat my sandwich and wait for him to get around to the Institute. After a moment's chewing he nods, and fills his lungs. "Our success had an unforeseen negative cost, it turns out. We as a population need victims to remain satisfied—perhaps you understand? In winning the war we were like the wolves who slaughter the flock all at once and starve the following season."

"It's a problem—" he seems overly fond of wandering analogies.

"We had our captives, as always, but these don't stay fresh. So then what—each other? We were not really suited to be each others' victims."

"And wouldn't your numbers dwindle pretty fast if you were all after each other?"

"Exactly."

"So what did you do? Did you attack your neighbors, then?" I'm surprised at myself; I'm entering into the spirit of the dilemma somehow.

"No! No! Godavia is not at all equipped for war of that kind. And as for anything clandestine, well … what little our kidnappers bring back is of highly unsatisfactory quality. With such rough terrain on all sides, we can only penetrate so far over our borders undetected. Someone will now and then bring in a goatherd or something but these mountain people are far too coarse a fodder for our purposes—we're looking for a *refined* sensibility you see, someone with the imagination and sensitivity to really experience to the fullest what's being done to them, you understand."

"I don't suppose importing … good people … has been considered?"

"Our neighbors are not blind," he says with finality. "And as for appeals to more far-flung places—what possible reason could anyone have for moving here, when we can barely find jobs for our remaining population?"

"And so, the Institute … ?" I feel I'm losing the thread.

"Yes. We have found ourselves in the embarrassing position of having to teach some of our own people to be good. Given the complexion of our character, unfortunately, we're not really certain how to go about doing it—hence this Institute, our research, experiments …"

"All to figure out how to make good people—for you to play with?"

"Precisely. The implantation of conscience is a very fiddly thing, and so far we haven't quite got the hang of it … but progress is being made every day, I assure you. In fact, you were invited here in the hope that we might be able to interest foreign governments, or even dare I say private investors, in our discoveries."

Even though I am not exactly a 'good person', I have been thinking about the sorts of ruses that might be used to attract 'good people' to Godavia, and growing increasingly concerned. Now that I know I am here as a—goodwill ambassador?—foreign emissary?—I feel a measure safer.

"Shall we begin our tour?" Dr. Bondi suggests, rising. I follow him down the hall—behind me the male nurses swiftly pack up and remove the table and chairs. I try to get a better look at the pointed-toed slippers that are intermittently obscured by the heavy hem of his cassock. I know we are already below the level of the street, and Bondi's tour promises to lead me down further still. This level is almost all surgeries. We pass pair after pair of swinging doors that afford fitful glimpses of sky-blue tiled rooms centered on piston-mounted operating tables; surgeons are to-ing and fro-ing up and down the hall, but, despite all the activity, we occasionally pass timeless rooms in which solitary patients lie waiting and possibly forgotten on their tables, their eyes dreamily fixed on the talon-like lighting arrays suspended from the center of each ceiling.

"Forty-five tables, and over a dozen surgeons, all of them completely alive to the complicated pleasures of surgery. We firmly believe that behavior modification begins with body modification," Dr. Bondi says, "Do you find that suggestive?"

The question seems odd to me. "I am struck by your assumption that something as uh intangible and elusive as a particular moral state could be induced by physical changes."

"We understand goodness to be some variety of indisposition or handicap, by our best estimate. The good person is unable to do certain things, simply because they are ungood."

"But good people are also compelled to do certain things as well … and how can you program someone so as to react properly in every situation?"

"Excellent questions all currently under research here. In the case of compulsion, we achieve this using means that might be familiar to you."

We now walk swiftly past an endless series of windowless wards. In some, there are so many heavily bandaged patients that even with two to a bed, there are still some who are forced to lie on the bare floor. The sounds coming from the wards … "Some of them will go through dozens of operations in time."

"Is it mostly brain surgery you perform here?" I ask.

"That has its share, naturally, but there is a great deal more, we find, than brain business to keep track of in the conditioning of organic morality. The whole endocrine system, for example, offers us practically as many opportunities for research as does the nervous," he draws the collapsing curtain of the elevator closed behind us, and we begin to drop. "However, almost all subjects sent on from the surgical wing have received extensive nerve grafts, to give them the utmost possible sensitivity."

I am shown into a small niche in the curved inner wall of a wide and dark hallway. Through a thin window-slit I see ranks of kneeling figures sitting on their haunches; they lean forward, their heads thrust into a darkened alcove, their bare backs exposed to rows of obscure, shadowy things on a platform above and behind them. Whether they are people or machines, these shadows vehemently lash the bare backs with rods or switches.

"Is *this* what you were suggesting I would find familiar?" I ask, groping to loosen my collar.

"Yes. Like parents and teachers all over the world, we have observed the common truth that pain has this salubrious effect: it promotes docility."

The subjects cringe under the blows, but none cries out. I can hear only a salivary mewling sound—these beatings must go on for hours. Glancing at Dr. Bondi, I see his nostrils flare, and he inhales with relish and at length; as though the bracing sound of all those blows affects him like a breeze off the ocean.

I am surprised to note the rods made a dull thud instead of the harsh smacking sound I would have expected. "Mm," Dr. Bondi replies, "well they do toughen over time, even with the nerve grafts ... Let me show you more."

Back in the hallway, he pulls open two cupboard doors and together we peer into a pitch-black shaft the size of a missile silo, or larger, extending an indefinite distance up and down. I can make out dim ranks of downturned heads in separate alcoves regularly spaced along the length, and all around the circumference, of the shaft's wall—they are the exposed heads of the flogged subjects, that bob as they are beaten. Weird, larger-than-life figures hover in the center of the shaft, now and then floating over to one of the bowed heads, and drifting back again. As they draw near the walls, they begin to glow; as they fly back into the center of the shaft, where masses of them clump together like bees forming a new hive, they dim down and become completely dark. With a whistle, Dr. Bondi attracts their attention and a few swing in our direction. As it comes up to the cupboard door, I see it's a machine.

"It didn't take much trial-and-error to discover that paternal and maternal figures are as important to morality-inducement as the literature cracks them up to be. Now," with an effort he reaches into the void and pulls one of the things out into the light, "this is the father type—we call him a Corrector— and he is of course associated with an increase of punishment."

He's holding by the scrawny neck an enormous, rather exaggeratedly masculine figure, with a bristling, mop-like beard and a stern, angry face like a Greek tragedian's mask. After allowing me to inspect it briefly he releases the Corrector, which sails off into the dark again on its own. Dr. Bondi then plucks out another.

"And this," he says, "is the mother type—what we call a Calmer—who is associated with a reduction of pain."

The Calmer is a bulbous puppet, surprisingly voluptuous ... in fact, it seems to be a confusedly converted sex doll.

"You'll note the large, soulful eyes," Dr. Bondi says, pointing.

"Yes I was admiring them."

He releases the Calmer, which promptly vanishes. "Both puppets," he says, slapping glow-powder off his hands, "have generic features that synthesize a number of research-specified moral traits. This whole installation is one of our most successful, with a correction rate of over sixty-three, although I expect you're not interested in the technical details. Suffice it to say that, so far, the family approach has been found to work best; fathers and mothers applied in alternation during flagellation exercises. Brothers and sisters may be introduced in extreme cases. On the whole," he closes the cupboard doors, "a highly viable flexible modular discipline system."

The hall wraps around the exterior of the shaft for hundreds of yards before forking outward. A slightly rancid cloud of institutional food steams over us as we pass the cafeteria.

"So far," I say after clearing my throat with difficulty, "everything you've shown me seems rather more extreme than anyone could practically expect the population of even a small nation to stand still for."

"These extreme measures represent merely the first phase of the overall experiment ... all this simply enables us to perfect our methods and determine the limits to their application—our implementation of these measures among the general population will of course be much less radical ..."

"Well, what did you have in mind—something like additives in the water supply, or subliminal information released into the air?"

"No, we had in mind some sort of surgical procedure that could be performed shortly after birth, along the lines of circumcision, the effects of which might be furthered later on by booster injections—although I wouldn't rule out the sort of softer methods you've mentioned as a supplement."

The circular staircase, though narrow, is nearly flush with the humid walls of the shaft; the room we descend into is a long flat concrete box, wet floors and a smell of salt water, gurgle of drains. He shows me enormous glass-walled brine tanks with brass rivets—devil-fish lie in circular depressions beneath gratings at the bottom of each tank, periodically emitting plumes of ink that coil like smoke around suspended legs and bodies—patients at the surface submerged in restraints. We look up at their pale, naked limbs and tender, water-softened feet drifting just inches above the razory beaks that click against the grilles.

"The ink just makes them more suggestible. We find it far more effective than hypnosis in some cases ..." Dr. Bondi peers at the bi-lobed pupil of an aquatic eye, staring back through the squares of the nearest grill, "You know, octopi have very large brains for invertebrates ... if only they could talk!"

And here is a roomful of patients, thrown in with a heterogeneous jumble of babies and newborn animals.

"Well we're not at all sure how this works but 'goodness' also seems to have something to do with this tender, protective instinct associated with the proximity of weak and helpless things—our research has not gotten very far in this regard so we've kept our aims relatively modest for the time being—to observe whatever empathic osmosis is underway here and, once we've studied it, we hope to reduce a formula ..." Dr. Bondi trails off vaguely ...

An escalator, going down, so long in its tight rectangular mirrored shaft I can't see then end.

"I'm struck by the number of mental patients you have to work with here, doctor, considering Godavia's size—"

At this Bondi holds himself upright, turns and corrects me—"These are not mental patients! The Moral Institute is absolutely not a madhouse! All the persons subjected to our experiments are as sane as you and me—they have to be. The mentally ill are far too well insulated; they've already developed powerful coping mechanisms ..."

"Then these are all—*volunteers?*"

Dr. Bondi smiles—"Not volunteers, just unlucky."

Now a stonebound passage of rough gneiss blocks, pierced here with a heavy wooden door fitted in iron and a pair of small, barred windows. As we pass, a low dismal chanting is audible.

"Oh, that's where we train their clergy," he makes an offhand gesture, without stopping, "those patients with more intelligence than sensitivity we cause to become clergymen."

He heads for the elevator; I can't resist a peek through a barred window into the vaulted chapel behind the wooden door—and what I see ...

Later, in the elevator, Dr. Bondi elicits a confession from me about this clandestine peek—my pale face and gasping give me away. His only comment in response was, "All genuine priests are inhuman in some way."

And, after a pause, "I must say I've been admiring them myself—it's enough to make me wonder if I've missed my calling!" Chuckling nastily he steps into the deep plush of a velvet-lined vestibule and sucks water from the drinking fountain.

My eyes rest stubbornly on the back of his left shoulder as he walks ahead of me down a tapestry-muffled gallery. The sound of my voice is stifled, as though I were speaking through a piece of wood, but I keep plying the doctor with my questions.

"So, assuming your work succeeds and you begin to manufacture good people, would they then be established in good communities or ... farms?"

"Hm!" My question about farms amuses him. "Well, we haven't quite worked out what the social applications might be ... we're thinking that a 'castle versus hamlet' model would make a good place to start ... but I'm getting ahead of myself there."

Corridors, hallways. Our pace accelerates by imperceptible degrees until I trot after Dr. Bondi through increasingly narrow passageways. At one point I am treated to the unedifying spectacle of Dr. Bondi's rear end shifting in front of me as we crawl on all fours down an extremely dusty and litter-strewn metal duct.

Dr. Bondi nimbly straddles and steps through a ragged hole in a plaster wall; I follow and topple forwards off-balance onto a flagstone floor, dragging chunks of plaster and chickenwire down with me. Dr. Bondi is already nearly out of sight. After running for several minutes, I catch up with him just as he turns, evidently not having noticed my absence, to me with an enthusiastic glint in his eyes.

"Now you're about to get a look at something really special." He batters through a pair of swinging doors, palm outflung.

Wave of ammonia, inadequately masking a rotten smell. Here there are brilliant shafts of light punctuating an almost total gloom; I happen to be standing close enough to one of the walls to notice the wallpaper and a painting of a sailboat. Patients lie under powerful lamps … in the bright illumination it is only the contrast between their skin and the faces and hands of the attendants bent over each one of them that suggests to me their weird pallor. Now I can tell, they are all blue-grey, a little shriveled, horribly stiff. The attendants shake them and even slap them, stridently repeating—"Your name is so-and-so. You are in the Moral Institute. You are dead. Your name is so-and-so …" And the patients moan and roll their heads on their pillows, or make galvanic movements under the sheets.

"Our moral research with necrotized patients is unique," Dr. Bondi is saying. "You see our reasoning—to a certain extent or with regard to certain possibilities in life and behavior the good person is so-to-speak 'dead to the world'—in the extreme figure of the ascetic one sees this most clearly. Now these patients are actually dead; they have no appetites, no sensations whatever. By restoring this or that feature, or complex of features—a single sense, for example, or perhaps non-color vision combined with an appetite for food—we can see just what physical configurations of faculties are morally correct—and to what degree—and establish what are the most desirable necro-anaesthetic conditions.

"But what's more—this research has so many different applications a new one occurs to you every moment—often goodness involves looking forward to a posthumous time when one may look back upon the present with the emotional neutrality and possibly even disinterested and generally-adhesive goodwill of death. Here, we can actually *test* this idea."

Dr. Bondi turns to look at me and evidently fails to find a complementary enthusiasm to his own. He seems to want to bring me around to his way of looking at things, or to get me to share in the spirit of his work, and takes me by the arm, leading me eagerly through a rusty iron grating in a featureless stone wall.

As I look out directly before me, nothing but evenly-lit empty space receives my gaze. An arctic blast of air rushes around my pant-legs and flips up the edges of my jacket, frosts my cheeks with the moisture of my own breath—the draught itself is bone-dry. I tilt only slightly forward, to look down, and vertigo turns my knees and calves to melting water; I lean back and clasp at the perfectly smooth metal wall with my fingers. I find no handhold, but only smear the surface with oil and perspiration from my hands. I am standing on a little unrailed balcony, an irregular shelf of grid-stamped metal, suspended above a bottomless shaft. Dr. Bondi stands beside me, unfazed, and indicates the other two figures who sit with their backs to us, at the very edge.

"Now these two," Dr. Bondi shouts to make himself heard over the roar of air, "are among our most interesting and longest-lasting subjects. All their senses are occluded, with the exception of their ability to feel pain, so as to be correctable, and their hearing, so that they may continue to receive moral instruction."

Despite my terror, I study them from where I stand. Their bodies can only be dead—I think they have been eviscerated—but I see that some kind of posthumous growths of tissue have caked their faces like streaks of modeling clay, leaving only the bizarrely normal ears exposed on either side of their misshapen heads.

"The Calmers castrated them, removed their arms, and their legs were rendered useless by injections, to keep them from getting excited and groping about on the platform. Having arms is often inducement enough to use them, and we don't want any unnecessary movement up here."

A long time seems to go by.

"Their legs were left on, to give them something stable to sit on."

"And those?" I somehow ask, pointing to the syringes driven into the sour, blackened wounds in their shoulders, "Sedatives?"

"Sedation of dead patients is unnecessary," is the terse reply, "that is a preservative."

I look for a few minutes more at those unhealable wounds.

Dr. Bondi brings me back through the wall, and as my vertigo abates I nearly fall forward onto him. As he waits for me to compose myself, I whitter a half-conscious question, "Why a shaft?"

Why the shaftscape? It's a kind of heaven—I mean it's what heaven is supposed to be like, isn't it? I think it's a rather good impersonation; the verticality, the regularity, the order, symmetry, the exalted altitude ..."

I begin to suspect the doctor's dissatisfaction with my response. When he suggests we move on, I agree too eagerly; given the smell, I am not much interested in lingering there.

We turn into a spacious, well-lit cubicles and offices.

"Unfortunately I'm able to show you only a fraction of what we are doing here." With this, he grandly presents me with the key to the Institute—gold-plated and the size of a baseball bat.

"We have dozens of them—but they are all real keys … That one opens the third street-level door on the Institute's western side … And may I take this opportunity to compliment you on your Godavian—you speak like a native."

"Oh, well, I had only enough time to study the little phrasebook you sent me … I can't believe I speak as well as a native like yourself …"

"—Oh I'm not Godavian; I was born in Rome."

We pass another drinking fountain.

"I take it from your last name that you're a countryman of mine?" he asks as suddenly I find myself back in the lobby.

"… No," I reply, "actually the origin of my family name is shrouded in mystery you see one of my paternal ancestors was orphaned in the American civil war—"

"Yes yes I'm sure it's very interesting but it's getting late and I have an appointment. Perhaps some other time."

Even though it is nearly midnight and overcast, the streetlights are all still unlit.

The Firebrands of Torment

From the *Tuey Monthly Occult Index* #137 (August 1948), entry by Arthur Hennepin Tuey:

"CHALMERS, Halpin—He who gave us so much in life left us less than nothing in death. Despite the lapse of twenty years, the mind still reels at Douglas' ham-fisted 'investigation'. But where has the common outrage of our community found expression in action? Finally, it is left to Tuey to put aside his infirmities and probe the matter personally.

"How many of our number have been dismissed and ignored as 'unstable'? How many persecuted outright as lunatics? The memory of Halpin Chalmers has been slandered and his work belittled almost as a matter of course. His stature in the field and the significance of his discoveries need no defense here. But the recurrent question of madness, especially with regard to the Liao drug, does demand our attention. Was Chalmers 'slipped a mickey'?

"An associate of mine, whose haunts include the Chinese neighborhoods of New York City, agreed to run this matter to ground for me. He visited as many traditional Herbalists as he could find, and I append here his account of a typical exchange:

'I asked about the Liao drug—a half-concealed snicker was the only reply.

"'What's funny?" I asked.

'Grinning, he exchanged a few words with a colleague somewhere at the back of the shop, a man I could hear but not see. The one at the counter seemed to be asking—should I tell him?

"'I don't understand," I said.

'He smiled and said, "Mister, you don't know what you're talking about."

'There was a pause. He kept on smiling.

"'Well are you going to tell me?" I asked.

'He snickered again and held up a finger. "Wait. I'll make you some Liao."

'He went down to the end of the aisle where the least expensive items were, and without taking his eyes off me took down five bottles. He brought them back, mixed some of the contents without weighing them, and pushed the blend toward me on a fold of paper.

"'Liao,' he said.

'Then, he went back to the end of the aisle, still looking at me and smiling, took down five other things at random, mixed them, and pushed the blend toward me on the counter, next to the first.

"'Liao,' he said. "Four thousand!"

'Then he leaned forward and said, "Confidentially, 'Liao' is Chinese Herbalist for snake oil. For tourists only."'"

*

"Don't be an asinine old woman!" Chalmers was saying. He wore a mildly disappointed and superior expression. "Nothing that you can say will induce me to stop now. I entreat you to remain silent while I study these charts."

Frank remained silent and stared at the clock on the mantel. Chalmers remained motionless and bored into his papers with his eyes. There were a series of primer images, designed to advance him in regular steps to the last, operative diagram of a single four-dimensional figure. He felt the iciness of its abstraction stitched in silver blazes behind his eyes—he cleared his mind and settled into a null state, the lines of the figure turning into sight-lines and then into time-lines. How long he had stared he did not know. He was breathing long vapor trails in time. The box with the Liao pellets seemed to twist into view off to one side of the desk—it was open. With a convulsive gesture he plucked up one of the pellets and swallowed it; it grated against his dry throat, his Adam's apple pressed against his high collar. The clock, whose sound seemed to emanate from somewhere behind him, suddenly fell silent.

He looked up to see Frank coming toward him with a solicitous, disapproving look. Frank's body yawed weirdly in the direction he had come, as if he were still in the intervening space.

"The clock has stopped," Chalmers said. His voice boomed in his ears. A sudden vertigo seized him and he spoke again, his voice rapid and quiet, to distract himself. The room rolled like the deck of a swiftly-tilting ship.

"… It is beginning to get dark and the familiar objects in the room are fading out." He willed himself to keep talking; he tried to orient himself according to the protocols of the experiment. He had not failed to anticipate some disorientation—to some extent the pretense of dictation was to be his anchor in the present. Dimly aware of Frank shaking his pen and the thunderous loudness of its nib.

"… Everything is dark, indistinct."

Something crashed over him like a wave of liquid air and an impalpable metallic cold—Chalmers' form was an icy mold in space, he felt his outline become something tangible in transparent layers of sucking cold. In suspended time he felt that outline gradually pass into him as if were ballooning out in all directions, a sense of rising above the horizon of time. He was sitting at his desk, and Frank sat across the room bent—motionless—over his pad.

*

From the memoirs of A. N. Burton, forensic expert and consultant to the Providence police department from 1927–1931:

"Regarding the murder of Halpin Chalmers, there was no evidence to corroborate the so-called "cult" theory, although this remains among the more likely explanations. Sidney [county coroner at the time] asked me to look into the possibility of insanity, given the character of Chalmers' books and the circumstances surrounding is death; viz the plastered room, the notes found around the remains, etc.

"My first task was to read Chalmers' books. In my opinion, they were clearly the work of a psychotic, although not necessarily a dangerous one. From what few accounts of his character there are, I am not inclined to say that he was a violent or hysterical man, regardless of the circumstances of his death.

"Lacking much firsthand evidence, I resorted to genealogical research. I have always been a firm believer in the importance of hereditary factors in the development of mental disease. It was here that I made the most interesting discoveries. Chalmers had been raised in Providence by Hetty and Boone Chalmers of Waterman Street, but, owing to my association with the police department and the nature of my investigation, I was given access to city records of adoption proceedings dated 1898. Halpin Chalmers' real parents were a pair of Dutch immigrants named Helstrup, who lived in Providence for a time before moving to New York.

"... as far as forensic evidence of insanity was concerned, there was almost nothing to go on. I was able to discover only that Chalmers' mother, Ada, died in Bellevue in 1901. The cause of death was 'general paresis.' In those days, that was sort of a "code phrase" for tertiary syphilis, although I would hasten to point out that, lacking any medical records or documentation from the autopsy, it is impossible to say precisely what disease she had. However, the fact that she died in a mental hospital is suggestive: syphilis, in the final stages, attacks the tissues of the brain, producing symptoms of insanity including hallucinations and paranoia.

"If Ada Helstrup did have syphilis, it is not out of bounds to propose that she may have had the disease as early as 1890, when she gave birth to Chalmers, and, in that case, she would almost certainly have passed it on to him. The plot thickens when we consider that Georg Helstrup, whose autopsy records I uncovered, was completely free from any trace of the disease when he died in an accident in the Fall of 1905. He had remarried, and when his widow, Sylvia, née Bishop, died a few years ago (April 1930), she also exhibited no signs of the disease.

"Whether or not Ada Helstrup had syphilis or something else, she evidently contracted it outside of her marriage."

*

A conscious element in a still life, Chalmers was facing the door; unable to move his eyes, his range of vision was fixed, with Frank's downturned face barely visible in the periphery. With an uncanny feeling of coming to himself after an unknown interval, Chalmers again returned in his mind to the protocols of the experiment and tried to orient himself. Chalmers had no where yet to go. He was there, now to go. Frozen, with no physical sensation, he felt a cold bodiless panic, as if his mind were panting and groping in the dark—his panic had driven the diagrams out of his head; with a great effort he brought them up in his mind now as if on a movie screen. The dimensions of the room around him began to alter and he seemed to be teetering on the brink ready to slide off, his will to remain where he was manifesting as a kind of increased friction or adherence to the chair.

Chalmers sat frozen against the tilt of the space he was in and stared at the room, at Frank's absurdly calm face, and at once understood that the fall opening in front of him was where he was going. He could either pull back or fall forward. He could not remain clinging to the margin with an effort that was exhausting him.

Chalmers released himself and slid forward, the room around him veered past and disappeared into nothing.

There was no way to close his eyes. Open or closed, or eyes at all, there was no light, nothing but the sensation of a kind of angular momentum. Chalmers rambled faster and faster in his mind—where space is angular, it will converge at fixed vertices. Motion down an incline. The room had opened in concentric series in parallel, each one like a frame in a film. His eyes had wanted to focus on each at once. Rising above the horizon of time. His body was present to him but it seemed to recede to a vanishing point in the depth, which was all around him. Was he still dictating to Frank?

There was a wrenching sensation, another scene took shape around him, turning the corner he saw his mother as he remembered her, sitting in a print dress on the front steps. The street was dark, there were no lights in the street or on the porch, only moonlight. She sat smiling at him, resting one hand on her rounded stomach where she was pregnant with him. Above her on the porch he could see his father almost completely invisible in the shadows leaning against the wall between the door and the window with his head tilted back, motionless, and there was, Chalmers suddenly knew, another presence there on the porch in the dark by the wall where his father was but coming from the other side from his father, moving low and curling round his mother where he started forward to get it away, it was something. He shook and saw it was almost a huge flayed dog, in the pale light he could see it—a dripping carcass rolling a long black tongue in its mouth and reeking like an open sewer, the stink hit him in palpable waves and he felt his body recoiling—even looking at it made his eyes feel infected, his face and hands were scummed over, and this beast nuzzled around his mother familiarly and where its body touched her dress it left a smear, and it left a smear on her bare arm. His mother let it come near and smiled at it—Chalmers' stomach convulsed so hard he nearly fell forward and he was still watching, he watched as the beast pressed his paw on his mother's belly, the beast did it with a proprietary air— the beast laid its paw on his mother's belly with an obscenely proprietary air— it touched her belly and looked up into her face and she smiled at it and glanced up at Chalmers with uncannily bright and vivid brown eyes, her everyday brown eyes were uncannily bright and vivid and laughing and Chalmers saw a light on the porch, a little glow from his father's face as he gazed down with laughing brown eyes which were uncannily bright and vivid; because of course Chalmers' eyes were as blue as the blue eyes this beast laughingly turned toward him—Chalmers made a sound and choked at once on blue bile as his limbs and body erupted like a bursting cadaver, falling to his knees he split down his spine, his face screwed up with anguish as if it were being crushed by an invisible hand, the muscles locked and the eyes burned hot, his crying voice bayed, his eyes popped open in his reeking face out of a halo of spiraling blue talons and he saw the blissful family smiling at him— still jackknifing uncontrollably at the waist he lunged at his mother wanting to claw that gobbet out of her belly, and to gouge the grin off of his father's face—before he reached the porch the beast and his unbearable blue eyes was there between him and them—all the strength flowed out of him and seemed to puddle on the ground; the spiraling cloud of his body stopped, helpless and staring at the scene which refused to fade.

*

From Burton's memoir:

"The last piece in the puzzle—not the solving piece, just the last one—was a photograph I uncovered of the Helstrups. There was a very strong family resemblance between Chalmers and his mother, but none at all to his father. We can only conclude that Halpin Chalmers, and almost certainly the disease that killed Ada Helstrup, was the result of an extramarital affair. As to the identity of Chalmers' real father, no clue remains. We may only say with confidence that he had blue eyes.

"But we must lay alongside the question of hereditary predisposition or even brain disease the equally important question of the extent of Chalmers' own knowledge of this case. Needless to say, the devastating potential of these facts, the adoption, the affair, the possible profligacy of Ada Helstrup, the possibility of an inherited taint, might drive an already delicately-balanced mind over the brink. From the point of view of the forensic psychologist, the most crucial question of all remains unanswered: how much of this, if any, was known to Halpin Chalmers?"

*

Struggling through a dark morass—as he had been for infinite time. Streaks reflected from nowhere on the surface, the only light. Weighted down and exhausted with an eternity of floundering and useless wandering to no ready goal, relentlessly pulled along by no will of his own, through a slough of filth that closed over his head and swallowed him the moment he stopped. He would watch the dim surface rising away from him and in panic claw his way out again, breathing and choking and swallowing filth. Burdened with an exhaustion that ground down into his perforated bones he had to fight at every moment the desire to let himself go, release his grip, relax his body, and allow himself to be swallowed once and for all time, sink to the bottom and disappear in the mire. His body was spent, rotted through and hanging in rags, a nearly formless clot of corrupted flesh, cold and lifeless, animated only by its decay. He could feel the powerful, alien life of the decay in his arms and legs that convulsively dragged him forward and kept his head above the surface. The decay rode him like an animating parasite, satisfying itself endlessly on what was left of his flesh and vitality. Despite the fatigue there was only a sweet toothache pain in his bones; an abominable, mocking pleasure warming his rotting flesh as it bloated and sloughed off in thin sheets, with a little ooze of viscous blood.

There before him—strange empty white room with rounded corners, and a figure inside—a familiar little man. He watched that little man pacing self-importantly around the room and he flung himself forward, screaming and clawing he flung himself again and again against the tiny room. Suddenly a gap appeared and he was through.

*

Chalmers stood just inside the corner of the room, in a half-space protruding into the room from the corner. He looked at his hands and they were hands and they were clean. A moment before things had been different. He had plucked off the offending organ, not the eye in this case he had done the Bible one better, and had paused a moment to redecorate the old place. Now he placed his head in his hand and gazed at Frank sitting frozen on the other side of the room—what a face! Pink and credulous and empty as a store for rent. Chalmers ambled to his chair and leaned over the back with his forearms crossed looking at Frank with sardonic pity. Well, well.

Chalmers resumed his seat and leaned back. After a moment he stiffened and opened his eyes, fluttering the lids. "God in heaven!" he cried. "I see!"

"Chalmers—Chalmers, shall I wake you?" came Frank's voice.

Chalmers ranted and raved, an inspired performance, to say the least. At the end, he crawled on the floor and spat lather from his lips. Frank grabbed his shoulders shouting. Rather a bit over the top but Chalmers barked jerkily to cover the spasms of laughter that were convulsing in his stomach; he snapped at Frank's wrist and nearly gave himself the hiccoughs trying to contain himself. Frank kept shaking and chiding, and Chalmers gradually relaxed, allowing himself to collapse on the floor, hiding his face.

Chalmers asked for whisky. He raved for sheer pleasure. "They are lean and athirst! The Hounds of Tindalos!" 'Tindalos' was the piece de la resistance, a Greek flourish meaning 'Firebrands of Torment'!

Frank's scientific education had not included Greek: "A week's rest in a good sanitarium should benefit you immeasurably."

And there Chalmers simply let his head hang back and the laughter pour out. And after Frank was gone, he went on, helpless, breath after breath of laughter filling up a mouth that distorted and distorted and distorted …

*

"… I did not mean to offend you." Chalmers was saying. "You have a superlative intellect, but I—I have a superhuman one. It is only natural that I should be aware of your limitations."

"Phone if you need me."

The door closed behind Frank. Chalmers sat in the middle of the floor, then curled into a ball, eyebrows raised, exhausted and helpless in his hilarity tears streaked down his face.

"The Hounds of Tindalos!"

He had tried to put a stop to it all when he first knew and lunged, but had been stopped instead. He had found his second chance in future time, but he would need to complete the gesture from this end, to bring both ends of the same story to meet, or should it be said, to bring together both rays at a common vertex. But there must be no interference from the family quarter so to speak. The family might not understand so to speak. That one would try to stop him again. He looked at the now weirdly-rounded room.

"Now I'm safe," he thought, and rolled on the floor again.

Chalmers watched the night fall through the newly oval windows. Some people bicycled by the window. The day's clouds swept by in much the same way. He enjoyed waiting. After it got completely dark he lay on the floor and doodled—what would they make of these? He scribbled note after note, frantically exaggerating his handwriting and collapsing in little fits with increasing regularity.

Suddenly the earth shifted, the ground bucked and the whole building shifted violently—Chalmers had never felt an earthquake before, but smiled up at the cracks that snaked in the plaster. When the quake was over, not a piece had fallen. He'd seen to it.

Chalmers rushed to the wall, where the edge would be, and as if inside it he felt the heat and onrush and the futile ragings—

"Sorry, but this is my room!" Chalmers said with a razory grin.

Not for long, but long enough. Calm returned, the onslaught was over, the gap in time had opened. Chalmers sat in the middle of the floor. His head began to nod, chortling bobbed up his throat, he took a sheet and wrote—

"Good God, the plaster is falling! A terrific shock has loosened the plaster and it is falling. An earthquake perhaps! I never could have anticipated this. It is growing dark in the room. I must phone Frank. But can he get here in time? I will try. I will recite the Einstein formula. I will—God, they are breaking through! They are breaking through! Smoke is pouring from the corners of the wall. Their tongues—ahhhh—"

—and at the last he flung it into the air on spiraling gales of hysterics rolling on the floor and clutching his stomach with both arms. Then, grinning, he got to his feet and casually stripped himself, throwing his clothes—well, not into a corner perhaps but away at any rate. He took up his hammer, and knocked away the plaster here and there, where the mood took him. The fragments he arranged on the floor, where he will wait, where he had seen himself waiting. Chalmers paced the unlit room.

Something is glinting in one corner. Chalmers looks more closely—the lines of the ceiling and the upright angle of the wall drop away, sight-lines into a deep distance, and where they converge there is a minuscule figure, loping on all fours, racing toward him with shining eyes. As Chalmers continues to look, the figure grows larger bit by bit, seeming to accelerate—when the eyes are near enough to recognize and the abyss before him has become a mirror, he gazes back at himself, Chalmers calmly moves to the center of his triangle to wait.

For No Eyes

Above me, at any moment, the wall will give way—and beneath me where I sit and flourish my pen—I'll stop a moment and flourish it   again ... another moment gone forever—I've never wasted time so voluptuously, the grand spenders are at their most profligate when they are almost bust—and there are fewer moments left now—and now still fewer—beneath me where I sit, in almost no time at all, I expect to feel a sudden shock—I've never felt an earthquake before, it promises to be quite a new experience for me—I expect the ground will drop all at once and throw everything into a satisfying disarray, as if this neighborhood were so much old rubbish on a bedsheet—a bedsheet suddenly seized at the edges and snapped. I am near the window—if I am immobilized by a falling beam or something, I will see it when it comes—I will be sitting here writing, and then a rumble coming up from nothing and everywhere terrifyingly fast, the earth will buck us off its back like so many fleas, lights will go out, commotion outside—that will only grow, the wind will rise and the rumble will not fade to complete inaudibility and by then I will be getting my first glimpse ... true to the stories I will be unprepared, I will scream the loudest, because what all will be combined in that scream for me—

We had decided not to write, no one, not a word, not so much as a shared confidence between a man and his diary, for fear of this and that—we kept our secret and all our promises, every one. We kept the one promise that no one has ever kept before, a promise kept only once, and remembered only here in this little hour I'll spend joking with these unreadable pages, my eyes are rolled back in my head and streaming, I'm not reading ... let the pen write, it's perverse to want to, perverse not to—

In my chest, there is an intimate little fold, where I feel it chime, against the palpitations of my heart there is the stronger pulsation of this, for all that as gentle as a billow of air, a throbbing note, like a ringing bowl, a blurred mouth that is bowed into an ellipse first this way then that. We called and it answered it answered—with a glorious lapse in silence after our call it answered us all the greatest joy that almost made us forget our grievances with this toy city—I know I forgot why, what reason I could have had, none of us had anything like a good reason, as if there were reasons—that answer was our reason—what was it?—at last a *good reason*! We called again and then again again only for that, when it would answer, out of shuddering silence our voices had cleared—now to *see it*, is all—we all had to see it ... I can't wait to see it—I can't wait to see what it's like, unlike anything—its answers were unlike anything—

To call to it, to come, again and again, months and months, until the last time we called to it, only thirty minutes ago we finished, surprised to be finished so soon, we found ourselves at the end, the last breath of the last syllable still trailing out—we had not been stopped—no one knew to stop us—any one of us could have sabotaged it with no more effort than is required to shout—or with no effort at all, by keeping silent—but we were all borne along on the gusts of it like obliging dust-devils and we were through before we knew it—what could have been averted with no more effort than is required to shout or simply to keep silent we had made *fact*—it is *fact*—it is *fate*—it is impossible to stop, it will come, it is coming *now*—we were one moment so many shabby lunatics—we were pitiful delusionaries—we were resentful tatters of urban marginalia fit for the looney bin but *we have rather a secret now* ...

not for long—it started right away, it picks up momentum every moment— the throb that drowns out my pulse is answered by the things around me, the melody on one instrument—is taken up gradually by the orchestra—and embroidered—back and forth—between the soloist—and the orchestra— complicating the refrain—and multiplying its dimensions—the wind is picking up the harmony chords in the basses—this music, the more solid it gets is a sensation I'm not bothering to describe—the theme is the last autonomous human act, the last historical act, and, insofar as it was ever possible, the last act any human one will ever take, ever *took*, then, to decide his fate—

already stirred, reflected in the things around me and in myself, we are neatly wrapped up into a funeral chrysanthemum by its stirring, stir up banked down unimaginable force boil out from under a world's burden of time—time nearly gone—it was little enough to do—by no means impossible though we're only human—fraternity of reeking alleys—society of derelicts in our pastoral of trash—partisans of decrepitude and irrelevance in hiding in plain view—in subway switching houses and tenement wells, and above it all—one atom and a city is gone—this atom among atoms writes from the book of atom—perhaps it may not look like anything—we may be the only ones to notice ...

none of us knows what to expect, though I expect the earth to buck and the wind to blow—what else is there to know, but that we called—it answered— nothing is going to keep me from seeing what it's like—farther away I seem to be now going down the funnel of a funeral chrysanthemum folded out of a warp of finest threads—these threads are clear—they sound where it pushes its *wave* before it and drift up here, accumulate like the deep clear wall below the wave, in dead silence, appears, the world's edge—then the wave ... breaks—

I'm thinking of stories here and there that I read forever ago and time and again—the type of story that would end in fragments trailing off in italics—

I notice—gradually I notice—that I am beginning—very gradually—to trail off—I should start writing in italics now—

it still seems quiet—

I'm waiting and listening—

I leave a gap here—

I hear it's starting my little moment left as something familiar to myself or dead all the same should I die this was all I wanted—to live this hour—with this throbbing note in me and this music rushing up impossibly fast—my last joke to an empty house as something familiar to myself or happy to die nobody will laugh at what no eyes will read except me of course I'll go on laughing

[Editor's Note: I cannot account for this material; I know nothing about it; I cannot say anything about the author or attest to the reality of the "cult" (for lack of a better word) that he seems to describe. Groping in the obscurity of a complete lack of evidence, there is no reason to assume the existence of either, although the passage which suggests that "it may not look like anything" raises certain doubts.]

He *Will Be There.*

My friend and fellow writer Joe Pulver asked me to contribute to a King in Yellow tribute volume (still in the works), and this was the result. While I enjoy the bizzarrerie Chambers' work, here I was trying to steal a Ramsey Campbell atmosphere, at least in the city scenes.

He Will Be There

For Joe Pulver

I went to visit my brother in the morning, passing a house on fire, further down my street. Here and there, among windows that were as calm and everyday as could be imagined, there were scorched and broken windows from which long flames were leaning. The air was full of smoke, that made my eyes water and turned the sky over my head the color of clotted blood, and as I reached my car I was lightheaded from the narcotic smoke of the burning house. Though I drove with my windows wide open, I was unable completely to rid myself of the odor of that narcotic smoke, and my vision swam, the road waved.

My brother Lewis lived alone in a slovenly apartment, which was incongruously small for the monumentally immense building that housed it. I had helped him move his few things there, after he was released from the hospital, but for all that, his apartment resembled a hospital room, and smelled like a hospital room, and the building looked as if it might have been a hospital in the past. Lewis was unable to work, and lived on a small stipend from the family trust, that I arranged and managed for him.

We met at the door and he sat on his bed by the window, where the very strong light nearly hid him from view. He was pale and lean and wore a white shirt, and grey trousers; he had no color of his own to speak of, he looked like a hazy photograph. He looked like someone out of a lost photo album, or like an expatriate scoured clean and blank by very foreign places.

Our conversation was desultory at first and there were many long pauses, as was commonly the case. The last time we had met, he had been reading Eusebius, and I asked him about it. With his back to me, facing the window, he said, "My religious practices have changed."

I asked him what he meant. He did not answer without letting a certain amount of time pass, as he always did when preparing to speak at any length. His voice elbowed its way in between the random noises the other apartments made.

"I've discovered a series of hand gestures," he said, and began to demonstrate them for me. He knitted the fingers of both his hands upright two inches in front of his stomach, the fingers held out stiffly and the thumbs curving upright; then he knitted his fingers a second time, at the final knuckles, and held his hands palm up and curved before him with his thumbs pointing forward, and so forth. As he performed these and other gestures, he explained in the flattened manner that was normal for him, "Nothing began with the word ... by performing these gestures with concentration, anyone may obtain enough truth as is required ... if you sat with them long enough, everything else would follow—come to you, right at your kitchen table."

He continued with his hands for some time, then stopped and loosely clasped them together in his lap, and smiled up at me. This was unusually responsive. I sat down near him.

I opened my mouth and wailed ... I allowed the sound to pour from out of my mouth, ringing in the narrow opening of my back teeth, with my shoulders back and my arms curled up loosely, like the wings of an unfledged chick. At times my eyes were screwed shut and at other times they would open, and I could see Lewis watching me with rapt, shocked attention. The sound I made only seemed loud, it would certainly not have been audible outside the room, but it was almost like a third presence in the room with us, it sounded nothing like my ordinary voice; the stress, and the concentration, were taxing and I felt the great pressure in my head but I enjoyed the effort, even though it made me lightheaded, and it wasn't long before I believe I almost hallucinated. I daydreamed that something like the colorless light of an alien sun was rustling through Lewis' room ... harsh and cloudy at once, like the light in a crime-scene photograph. I stopped when my throat began to ache, and Lewis asked me about it.

"The last time I visited the family plot," I told him, "—this must have been a month ago, I go every month if I can—"

"—yes," Lewis said.

"Anyway, I was heading back for my car when I thought I heard a man keening in an underground vault, because I was passing a row of them when I heard it. I listened through a sort of a stone pipe out the back of the crypt, and it stopped. I left, but I couldn't stop thinking about that sound, the way that man's voice *rang*, like a bell. I realized, a few weeks ago, that I could try to reproduce it—I could make my own chest something of a crypt for my voice to resound in, and my throat would be the pipe, and so went from there."

"... Did you know you were making two tones at once?" he asked.

Lewis seemed unusually alert that day, so I decided to broach my subject to him, as to my specific reason for visiting him.

"I was wondering what you'd make of this," I said, and handed him "*The King in Yellow*," which was a play that had been sent to me in the mail by someone I didn't know, who had left no name or return address on the parcel but encouraged me, in a short note, typed, to mail it to someone else, at random if necessary, when I was through with it; I assumed that I had been chosen at random, since I didn't know anyone really. I had read it, and I wanted Lewis' opinion.

Lewis started reading through "*The King in Yellow*" while I puttered around in his kitchen and cleaned up. Now and then he would point to a name and ask "How would you say this?" without looking up from the page. When he was roughly done he looked up at me with his very vivid eyes and smiled sheepishly.

"I think this is a little beyond me, Bill," he said.

We decided to go into the city together.

*

Lewis and I dropped down into the subway and stood at one end of the platform gazing back into the tunnel's brown shaft, tilting down out of sight. The air of that day was already heavy with humidity and too warm, down in the tunnels the air congealed in a hot stinking ooze. Perspiring, we both walked up and down, I would have been panting if the air had been more wholesome, but the onrushing train, whose squinting, myopic lights were suddenly visible in the far distance, was pushing a column of miasmic air in front of it; the artificial wind bathed me in a reek of urine and stagnant water, and a cloying odor of fresh paint thickly exhaled by the newly-retouched girdered columns. As the train groaned along the platform, Lewis was scanning the goods at the kiosk. He bought a lighter and some hard lemon candy, although I had never known him to enjoy sweets. We sat side by side in the first car, the seats were yellow orange and brown.

The window opposite us was scraped by the shallow darkness of the tunnels between the stations; our two faces were hopelessly lost in it, faint like the flames of candles and dark at the centers, so that only the surfaces of our faces reflected light. Our eyes were four holes in a canted row. Even when the sun is shining on the ground above, there is no sunlight underground. Except what is re-radiated from human skin, that shines in gold or fluorescent color, because a human will keep and emit his sunlight. My brother and I could only be seen in subway light; we had no light.

A large man with extremely dark skin, in a suit and carrying a zippered Bible boarded the train and sat near us. The ebb and flow of the starts and stops—when he left the car a few stations later, Lewis nudged me and nodded toward him.

"Uoht," he said, in a richly humorous voice. We chuckled over that together.

Lewis silently opened and steadily ate his box of lemon candy. I didn't share them—there was no air conditioning in the car and I was constantly wiping the sweat from my face and neck onto my hands and wiping my hands on my trousers. An old man decked out in a scarecrow get up mish-mashed from castoffs trudged to the front of the car and sat by the driver's door. I covered my nose with my salty hand. He fished a short butt from the pocket of his dirt-stiffened sweatshirt and lit its blackened end from a matchbook. I looked at Lewis; sweat ran in streams down his impassive face. The old man crushed out his butt after a few puffs and pocketed it. The train ebbed and banged back and forth, whinged and started again. Then it stopped somewhere, between stations, and we sat waiting, the window opposite us was empty except for an ugly sodium light; the air stood completely still. I glanced at the old man. He was holding his brown plastic shopping bag in front of his face, he had been puking beer into it silently. He stared at the empty seats opposite him with resigned animal calm and now and then lowered his head, soft patter of fluid in the plastic. Watching him, I became calmer, too. The train rolled forward and, when its doors hastily rattled apart, I pulled Lewis with me onto the platform.

We transferred to an express for the downtown stops, into a car that was already beginning to fill up. At the next stop it was filled; we stood by the doors, forced to either side by crowding passengers, and shifted with the rest of the human heap as the driver jerkily accelerated and decelerated. Lewis and I could only eye each other around a haphazard barricade of shoulders, upraised arms, and restless eyes, faces and heads in every direction, an orange ear glistening a few inches from my nose.

I ascended to the street already weary, but Lewis was in the mood to go on walking. As we were disgorged from the underground a garbage truck hurtled past belching a black plume of diesel exhaust, and trailing after it a hot, rancid stink that hung in the air and clung to our clothes. My brother and I swam through a morass held fast between high buildings, air churned only by braying traffic and the occasional surprise updraft of subway air through sidewalk gratings as trains hollowly roared past below. We were walking too slowly to merge successfully with the fast-moving pedestrians, who filled the pavements and spilled out onto the avenue in a bulging motley centipede of scissoring legs. The side-streets were emptier, but the little shops that lined them were not bland and indifferent like the boulevard shops; these little shops peered at passers-by. A billowing hood of warm, beery-smelling moist air, laced with musty cigarette smoke, suddenly washed down on us, and, as I glanced into the bar through its open door, I could see its sallow, sticky-faced personnel following us with their eyes, as if they had been angrily waiting for just such a couple of scarecrows to amble by.

Together, we hurried on toward the next avenue. Lewis glanced at me and said, with a limp grin, "The scalloped tatters of the King in Yellow must hide Yhtill forever."

I nodded, and grinned weakly in return. In the grey lobby-windows of a building under construction, our reflections appeared, sliding beneath the thickly-scribbled layer of dust that still coated them: two long lean phantoms, our heavy hands hanging down and our heavy feet tramping in battered shoes, and past our shadowy eyes, in the dim light inside, were visible a floor drifted in white plaster-dust, ladders and heaps of abandoned tools, wires and corrugated metal hoses drooping from the ceiling, murky columns and doorways splitting the space into dozens of stealthy paths into warm darkness smelling of paint and fresh concrete. I had the impression of a man in a bathyscaphe drifting past a shipwreck, the meager reach of my gaze brushing something submerged, uncanny. Lewis was looking, too.

A trance unfolded and made us walk without pausing, trailing through the streets as if the city was the shipwreck over which we drifted. The foundations of the buildings leaked urine in thin streams slithering to the gutter, and the sweat of air-conditioners spattered us. Washington Square swirled up around us, clamoring with blazing crowds. I remembered that the Square had once been a potter's field, and for a moment I mistook the crowd for a crowd of another sort. My thoughts were disjointed, heat-scrambled, weaving and tired. The Square lurched sluggishly after us, then disappeared again.

Finally, I leaned against a wall slick with the oils of its painted bricks and shook my head so as not to collapse on the filthy sidewalk. Lewis supported my arm as inconspicuously as possible; he seemed to expect an attack, provoked by my show of weakness. He hurried me around a mound of drooling garbage bags into a building—we were not accosted. The elevator opened on an empty corridor on a high-numbered storey, white walls, blue metal doors, thin institutional carpeting, detergent smell. I had begun to revive a little in the cool air; I knelt on the floor and sucked at the drinking fountain, so empty I could feel the cold gather in my stomach, until I was full, and then lay against the wall with my feet out before me. Lewis wandered up and down, exploring the various rooms, while I gazed up at the cork ceiling panels and the fluorescent lights. Time passed. We were on the street again.

The sun was setting, and we made our way to the park. The motionless air did not grow any cooler ... The paths, even the unpaved paths, were teeming with people, and the benches were all full. We found a tree and cleared away the trash at its base, lay against it looking up through the branches. Vacated by the sun, the sky had turned the brown-grey color of a pig wallow, and I couldn't tell whether it was clear or overcast. The city around us salivated lurid patches of horrid orange sodium light, and I still thought I smelled something rancid in the unbudging air. Lost in these swollen crowds could be any number of dead, any number of simulacra unnoticed. Had one of these passers-by mailed that play to me?

Together, my brother and I watched the night fall, while I felt the knotting in my aching muscles, the stiffness in my neck against the brittle tree. Lewis held out his hands in indication of the city and repeated with conviction, "The scalloped tatters of the King in Yellow *must* hide Yhtill forever."

Mysterious as this was, it was certainly no mystery to *me*, for I was nodding at its plain sense.

*

Waking with the sunrise, lightheaded and floundering on joints that felt battered out of shape, and without bothering to pull the leaves from my hair, I trailed after Lewis, following him back to the subway, back uptown to his apartment. I washed, then he washed, by the time I had dried myself I was sweating again, and we both emerged into the street still damp, my hair lying flat and slick on my head, smelling of Lewis' cheap perfumed soaps.

I led Lewis to my car. I drove from block to block while he sat with his elbow out the window; his eyes scanned the sidewalks. After a while, we passed a school with a busy playground, and circled round to the anterior side where there was a sunken alley between the brownstone school and a tufted lot bordered with a reclining slat fence. Lewis drew my attention to a boy evidently waiting for someone at the mouth of the alley. We stopped and working together collected him without difficulty. Lewis held him on the seat between us, his hands on the boy's shoulders, patiently pushing the struggling boy back into the seat. The wind rushing in the windows dampened and dispersed his cries for help; we were already on the highway.

The shouting lapsed but the boy continued to struggle. We neither had spoken. The boy was crying and his sobs permitted him to speak only with difficulty; he spoke a stream of questions and pleas. When he asked where we were going, I interrupted him.

"*He* will be there," I said.

The boy did not quiet.

Several miles down the road I pulled off onto a dirt track and circled round a stand of trees, throwing dust into the air. I stopped in a heady blond meadow of tall grass in a ring of black trees, broken in one spot by the thin bank of a faceless lake. A collapsed barn stood in the meadow like a giant, flaking ribcage, busy with flies. I stopped the car and Lewis and I brought the boy with us into the hissing meadow. As we neared the barn the ground grew rocky, the grass thinned, and there was a rust-tracked slab of concrete where a bench or trough had once been bolted, lying at a distance of several yards from the barn. I held the boy at that spot while Lewis went behind the barn.

The sun was setting behind the lake, pink and then red, and I saw no reason why the lake should not extend beyond the horizon, and should not therefore abut on another shore, in another world; it in fact looked precisely as if it did.

Lewis returned from behind the barn, carrying a metal chair that was more rust than metal, flecked with white paint, and a dented gas can, which I could hear slosh as he brought it near. The boy nearly pulled free of my distracted hands with a sudden lunge, but I collared him and held him again, his screams renewed. Lewis placed the chair on the concrete slab and sat in it, raised the gas can over his head and doused himself, pulled the lighter from his shirt pocket and, leaning forward, touched its flame to the cuff of the right leg of his trousers—he was ablaze before he straightened his back again.

He sat erect with his hands on his thighs.

The boy choked and stood paralyzed. Then his chest started to heave and he screamed and struggled but he could not get away from me; I held him in such a way that he could not turn his head. His shrieks grew deeper and wilder, and I knew my fear that he would not understand was groundless.

I watched my brother vanish through overflowing eyes and though my vision shuddered I saw him swathed from head to toe in yellow draperies of flame, his erect head crowned with long golden tongues touched with pink from the parallel conflagration of the sunset. For a moment, he stared gigantically down from his high seat, so that even the boy was silent before the awful gaze of the man-shaped shadow in the wind-whipped fire. My brother died, and a long, hollow wail, of two tones, broke free of my throat, like a beam projected into the clear pink sky from out of my mouth, directly over Lewis' head, now sunken on his chest. A few moments more, and the fire consuming my brother was the only light …

There were police cars gathered at the entrance to the school but the alleyway itself was still empty. I stopped there.

"You will see him again," I said. "… and me, never again."

He stared, then sprang out of the car, running down the alley, his head in his hands. I saw his head crowned with his upright fingers, and I heard his yellow voice. When he was gone, I pressed the accelerator and the car leapt forward, the passenger door swung shut.

I Will Teach You.

At one point, Bob Price was contemplating a collection of ghoul stories, and asked me for a contribution. Pickman is the center of interest in "Pickman's Model"; he preserves his composure extraordinarily well considering the fact that he routinely works with cannibal monsters who seem to exist only in order to make a mockery of mankind. One of my favorite writers pointed out that all monsters have to start out human; their monstrousness lies in the fact that the humanity they once had was lost.

I Will Teach You

For you all—

This is my madman note that will tell you that I am gone. You know I have been gone already, for a long while. I wish you hadn't made such an effort to bring me back to you, or that you could have been successful. Every time I've tried to put pen to paper to write a comforting lie my hand falls away, fatigue pushes me back in my seat, I have no ideas, and no real will to lie. The truth is more interesting, it transpires that the truth is the most interesting thing. I know there will be lies enough after and that this note will undergo every kind of scrutiny without ever once being read frankly, but for all that I know I will be called a mentally sick man, if I'm lucky even a tragically mentally sick man or a man tragically stricken by mental illness as though it were a sort of a bug, as though I couldn't lucidly choose to go for my own reasons—for all that I know the kind of excuses that will be made for me, all the same I have the urge to *share*, for reasons I am just now beginning to understand. You and the others will certainly have to ask yourselves whether Hunold's disappearance was the first case—you will think about Hunold and me, and you'll be right, there is a connection.

I don't know how I came to be so far away from you. I've just glanced out the window and seen you come up the street, and I thought to myself, "That is my wife." Earlier I had been looking at the pictures on the mantle and I thought, "That is my son, the musician." I heard these words in my mind's ear or read them there in my mind, as though I were an agent assuming a foreign identity; but this agent has no prior identity, none now, none ever. I hear you come in and pass my closed door without making too much noise, you imagine things are taking their course as usual and you want to leave me undisturbed, and I thank you for that, but I find I can't imagine you to myself anymore, I can't see you in my mind's eye as you pass on the other side of my closed door, nor can I picture our son, whose name escapes me, as does yours. Where you are now, or where he may be, I can't imagine. I don't say these things to be cruel, I don't know why I say them, except to share them—I think also to show you what it's like for me now. But it's very important to me that you understand that I have no malice, no feeling. This started long ago and is no one's fault—it's interesting, there is no cause of any kind that I can find. From the outside, just like you, I watched myself becoming unlaced from the world, and floating on the surface of things I did not touch, and I didn't understand it, either. I do know that Hunold was not the cause—perhaps I was the cause of his disappearance, although for some reason I doubt that. Hunold was certainly not the cause, but now that I am in this state or

70

non-state it is Hunold who invites me to follow him. I leave here to join Hunold. You are right to believe that my fate and his are linked, are the same. You don't understand that fate, and you will finally call it something else—as you like. I only write because this is interesting, and you will be interested to read what I have to say.

You never met Hunold, you didn't know him. I suppose I was his only friend—although he is among friends now—but I saw him only at the college and occasionally at the cheap little cafeteria he liked. But Hunold never struck me as a lonely man, and he seemed to have no use for people. While he enjoyed passing the time with me I am as you well know not exactly a personable type myself. I remember Hunold telling me that he liked me for my "resigned attitude." I am sure you will recognize that. I can't say that I recall our dire conversations with nostalgia, or with pleasure—I admired the uncompromising way he would go on about death, about nullity. He would sift and resift his ideas, search out and eliminate anything consoling, so as to be left with only the starkest picture. He wanted to face the worst and be done with it. I had always felt that he would have come up against it sooner or later anyway, brooding and fear had already tethered him to that nothing long ago, but he had taken command of himself, and had made what would have been a precipitous and terrifying fall into a disciplined and rigorous interrogation of the facts. (I'm in fine form) He interrogated the echoes of his own questions—(not bad)

But I may never know what all this ultimately came to ...

Hunold had only one living relative, a cousin his own age or perhaps a little younger. He didn't speak much about this cousin but when he did I thought I could detect an unwonted warmth in him. Every now and then I would learn that this cousin was visiting, and Hunold wouldn't appear for a few days ... I remember how Hunold told me this, on a park bench. He had risen very early as usual and had walked into his parlor to see if this cousin was awake. He told me that he stopped in the doorway, and that he saw his cousin's bare feet resting on the arm of the sofa, and his ankles, protruding from his pant cuffs, looking very long and pale and thin, and he knew at once that his cousin was dead, even before he looked into his face, or shook his shoulders, or called his name. The doctor wasn't able to find the cause. Hunold related to me how he was told, bluntly, "Sometimes they just *go*."

I only discovered all this some time later—Hunold and I spoke together only rarely after the death of his cousin. For over a month or so, I knew only that some appalling change had come over Hunold; I had no idea he was distraught with his cousin's death. He was unapproachable then—I would sometimes see his few students grimly filing out after his classes looking as though they had spent the last two hours sitting up with a cadaver. Once I glanced in on him after his last student had gone. He stood by the window in the empty classroom, looking down at a street filled with striding people, alive, going about their business … I glimpsed his eye and I know what I saw snarling there—hate. Later, Hunold's mood seemed to improve and we exchanged words occasionally—then as he had previously he asked me to join him for lunch or to take a walk with him, something like that. I say his mood *improved* … but what do I know about it? I saw the ends of his mouth screwed up in a painful-looking grin and I heard him chuckle to himself, and now that dusky chuckle I hear at the end of every street and alley. We would walk together almost without speaking and I would see his eye graze on the passersby, or there was something in his eye or his look that grazed on them. And at the same time, there was something earnest and transformed in his face, as though he'd found religion. The last time we ate together I remember sitting by the dusty window with the sun glaring in, Hunold opposite me; we talked, and though he said nothing out of the ordinary there was something driven in the way he said everything, locked eyes with me.

After his disappearance Hunold was eventually presumed dead by the authorities, and I agree with them. Having removed his person from the scene, Hunold was now everywhere in the same way the dead are there to be seen in passing cars, windows, shop displays and sunsets, waves, weather, trees. I knew he would not be found and would not return, at least not to the life he had lived. But I really didn't know anything then. As you know I spent a great deal of time away from home and away from the college—I used to tell you that I had been walking when you would ask me where I had been, and this was the truth. I wandered with an empty head around town, I wandered especially in the vicinity of the cemetery. The crowds tired and deadened me; I wanted to be alone in open spaces. On my second visit I discovered the grave of Hunold's cousin, purely by accident of wandering at random. It was nearly engulfed in a clump of trees on a hillside near one of the borders of the cemetery—I stood over it blankly staring at the writing without reading it, noting only the name, and I had the impression I might be standing in Hunold's footprints. With the cemetery stretching off on either side, it seemed as though the horizon had contracted, that I was standing on the convex surface of a very small planet, my head thrust up into the atmosphere. I was a giant standing at the grave of a giant.

As I was leaving, I glanced back at the hill.

Later, on the street, what I had seen returned to me—I had seen people here and there, and noticed someone near the top of the hill, walking up the path that snaked past the grave I had just visited. As a numb feeling began to spread across the back of my neck, and the back of my head, I saw the tall man facing away from me walking with his hands at his sides and his fingers slightly curled in a way I was familiar with, his head, covered in dark grey close-cropped hair, was stooped, he was wearing the sort of dark loose suit that people are buried in. In my glance I had seen this man take two long strides approaching a little custodians' yard atop the hill, camouflaged by the trees and shrubs, surrounded by a chain-link fence with green laths woven in the links. As he came towards it I saw movement inside the enclosure through the small gaps in the laths, and the gate was abruptly pulled inward. The man who opened the gate gave the impression of being elderly, from where I was— nearly hidden by the gate he was stooped and hobbling, bald with protruding ears, all dressed it seemed in dark lichen-colored clothing and perhaps dark gloves, the bulge of his knee seemed to suggest that he was crouching which he was certainly not possibly he was wearing jodhpurs?—I saw him more or less in silhouette and I remarked hastily that he must have been a very vigorous old man, and blinked when I saw in my memory how, when the first man had slipped by him out of sight, the man in the enclosure had turned a little and removed his right hand from the gate so that the alarmingly thick arm dropped straight its knuckles almost brushing the ground. I walked robotically down the street with this image swimming too clearly in my eyes, nearly stumbled into the path of a car, and, after it had passed, I continued to walk in the same way, making excuses to myself and knowing all the time that I had seen no old man—that I had seen no man.

At the time you noticed the change in me, and how I forced you to accept my glib answers to your questions, the way I shrugged off your concern. I was not at peace with these things then, as I am now. You observed, with your customary acuity, that I was acting like the unctuous servant of an invalid master lying prostrate in a trance in some darkened room back of my face; I kept affairs moving smoothly, but admitted no one to see that diseased and enfeebled sleepwalker inside. Though I was divided in myself as to what I had seen and made every effort to quarantine this memory, of course I could do nothing to forget, do nothing to head off its little tricks.

Hunold had left no will, some little part of my mind said, why not take responsibility like a good friend should?

His neighborhood abutted on the cemetery. I remember the weather was hot and unusually dry, a dust sirocco scattered itself everywhere, the dust seemed to drop from the sun, fell burning in every corner. The streets were almost empty, and very quiet—Hunold's neighborhood seemed to hold a special attraction to elderly women, each boxed up in a tidy, quiet little house. I turned in off a blinding street and nearly collided with Hunold's landlady, an old woman in a shapeless blue dress. She coughed and complained to me about Hunold's departure as though he'd gone to spite her, but agreed with a wave of her hand to let me into the apartment.

Once alone inside, I stood just within the door like an idiot. I looked around Hunold's small, spartan apartment and asked myself incredulously why I was there. As I walked about the two rooms, brushing things stupidly with my hands, I felt that of all places this was the least imbued with Hunold's presence. These bits, the razor, the small shelf with its heap of books, the fork and dish, had nothing to do with Hunold and said nothing to me. I told myself I had wasted my time and lowered myself to this perhaps obscene intrusion, but I didn't want to leave right away. I found myself at the window, absently taking in Hunold's view, bordered by the fire escape. The yard behind the building was overgrown with rank weeds and many tall plants densely knitted together, I remember they were all very lush and green despite the brittle, drying weather. The wall bordering the yard on the left was little more than a crumbling heap of bricks. The rear and right side walls were in better repair—those bricks were grimy but in line. And in the far left corner I could see a white square block of concrete glimmering through the heavy foliage—there was a scab-colored manhole cover in it, that, from there, appeared to be only loosely laid over the hole. What might have been only the low shadow of the cover could also have been a little gap—perhaps the cover had been inattentively replaced by the last person to move it. An impression was forcing itself on me and I caught myself peering down at the bracken searching for anything like a track between the concrete block and the spot below the fire escape—I caught myself, and I stopped myself from thinking any more, and I removed myself from there.

You know that I was sent home several weeks ago from the college, that I had been to the hospital briefly, that I had collapsed. You knew that some special incident had caused this attack and you knew that I was not telling you the truth about my out-of-the-blue "fainting spell." All right. I was collecting my mail, sifting it on the spot, there was a blank envelope, I opened the envelope, I removed from it a page neatly cut from an art book on which was reproduced a certain painting. The painting, which you have not seen, depicted a huddle of some fellows let me say some creatures, not people, shall we say grave-robbing fellows, monsters, and they were sitting there in a crypt, and one held of all things a Boston guidebook in his hands or paws or so on, and was pointing to something, and these fellows were all laughing very heartily and wickedly and enjoying some sort of joke, and of course the joke is the title of the painting which I knew and which was printed in italics below the reproduction "*Holmes, Lowell, and Longfellow Lie Buried in Mount Auburn,*" and below that there was handwritten one of his favorite quotations which he had quoted to me several times, something someone had said about Byron that he had been one of the few to mock everything that was human, and the handwriting was familiar to me and I rather stupidly allowed that to alarm me.

I eventually returned to Hunold's neighborhood and wandered around the cemetery, you know that, and I would sit and watch the streets perhaps waiting to see him wondering if he might return from his disappearance whose nature I still refused to acknowl-edge obvious as it was. I watched the people in the streets around the cemetery and of course I thought about what I had seen, without acknowledging it, and about the painting, and I thought, "but wouldn't people have noticed something—how could-n't they?" and the next moment as I watched face after face drift by, it dawned on me—*"everyone knows ..."*

Of course people have noticed—I watched them, and not one ever glanced up at the hill bristling with graves in plain view, they kept their eyes lowered, obviously lowered. I can't say what made—makes—me so certain—but the impression was as sharp and clear and obvious as could be—Hunold had uncovered a secret, of course, but a secret known and kept by everyone, at least, everyone here. I saw it in their shadowy, ordinary, haunted-looking faces—a "fact of life" unacknowledged, no name or picture attached, something never thought, never dallied with, but whose presence is always felt—and what could they do about it? What could they do? What was there to do?

Young and old, and no matter what apparent differences, these mute witnesses had always the same faint darkness around the eyes, the same worn-out look, the same closed features. You know that look—you know it from me.

I first heard Hunold's voice some time later ... passing along as always I wandered until my legs swelled writing gets so tiresome after a while I was passing along and I stopped to throw something away or tie a shoe I don't recall—from the exposed upper portion of the basement wall nearby I could hear a voice speaking steadily, in particular in that steady measured soft calm way that only Hunold had. His voice was muffled by the brick but the tone and manner were his and there was something in the way he spoke though it was quiet that made the brick basement ring like a bell so that I felt the wall's hum in the air.

As I said I wandered everywhere in those days and all the different parts of the city slid by me like scenes projected on a screen, I mean I was floating along like a man in a current, in a river and so not in contact with the land sliding past me at all, and if I saw no "handholds" to catch on to but I did after all see all sorts of handholds flashing by, but I wouldn't grasp them, I let them go on or I let myself go on like that.

And I was always just seeing Hunold or just missing him, whenever my daydreaming would abate a little I would glance up suddenly and feel perhaps I had just missed him around a corner or entering a building, perhaps he had been sitting opposite me unnoticed and I would remember seeing someone seated on the train or in a booth in the cafeteria nearby out of the corner of my eye and wonder—had that been him? But I did hear him, first of all on a busy street near the college, I heard him say "There is more to life than life."

This I heard clearly, although he was nowhere to be seen. I heard the phrase again later, this time in the financial district where I had gone on some business or other I heard him speak again much as before "To be alive is to be dependent on others—to be alive is to be a slave—" he spoke at length, "the dead depend on no one and so the dead are free" and I was up and down the pavings of streets whose houses stared blindly at me like the crumpled impacted faces of corpses and days went by, I heard his mild voice always calm and patient still, explaining to me, quietly murmuring to me sharp and clear below the wailing operatic tenor on the café's PA, the louder the song the plainer Hunold's distant voice sounds its syllables beneath it like a carrier wave, "I will teach you to savor a mouthful of rotting meat."

I saw him again, you know, a short time ago. I had been kept late because I work so badly now, very slowly – I ended up alone at one end of the platform, which was empty owing to the late hour.

I turned around once and glanced back down the platform. The outline of the black circular tunnel mouth at the far end of the platform was irregular for some reason. I looked—protruding onto the platform, I saw a black sleeve with a white cuff and hand hanging from it, they shone white through grime. The man from the cemetery whom I had last seen walking up the hill and whose name you know was there just at the edge where I suppose he had come out of the tunnels that penetrate every part of the city, he wore a loose-fitting black suit and white shirt, black tie, the sort of suit men are buried in. I heard the voice very clearly making an invitation to me in echoes from deeper in the tunnels, baffled a little by the packed earth walls of huddled lightless burrows where the air is stale and still and foul ... and then the train appeared—there was nothing in its headlights. I boarded the first car automatically and the empty car slid into the tunnels. I was sitting by the window looking out at the other passages radiating out in the distance, seeing my ghostly face superimposed over them on the glass, outside I was scanning the tunnels calmly, for movement ... There was no sound except the rush of the train— the lights in the tunnels went out, the windows of the car went completely black, I was face to face with my reflection, then the lights in the car went out.

I've lost interest in explaining, and I don't know that what I've been writing here makes any sense. From where I sit, I can see the small garden-park opposite and a few dozen yards up from my front door. There are two trees on a little rise just short of the circle of light cast by a single lamp-post. I see now, dimly, planted between those two trees, a pair of shineless, scuffed shoes, and the figure standing in them with his hands at his sides. His bruised unblinking eyes gaze up at me.

The Night of the Night

… among these processionals is this described as the Night of the Night of those persons of jagged Ejve Biis whom we know for their ancestry. The Ejve Biis receive the ambassadors of their ancestors.

They retire in the evening with a great show of outdoor banqueting finished they retire calling loudly to one another and lie still until the last dimming of twilight's lamps departing from the windows of the houses of twilight without glass windows that shine with the lamps of twilight and dim with twilight until the last, when there are no more embers, the oil is cold, there is no wisp of smoke but just ashes, when there are only ashes, if all is in darkness then because the dark moon is in the sky, there is only the darkness to which they are accustomed, just then they rise and go out to the mountain of night, come out in silence to the mountain of night hidden by the dark moon they come out in silence and alone going along one by one where their paths meet in long lines they circle the mountain of night hidden by the dark moon and come to the peak without light and stand as though blind, darker set against the dark sky, the idol of moons is there—

Beneath the gaze of the blind idol of moons they turn invisible when the priest speaks, they come to the idol of moons and when the dark moon has passed behind the idol of moons and is obscured by the idol of moons the priest comes from beneath the idol of moons and speaks, says 'It is night for Night,' they turn gale-eyed for dances and sing with strident wails into the sky unheard by sleeping Night, dance unseen, kiss in the dark like their young one another and each other in the dark like shadows in shadows clear as water and invisible, and with their priest they sing or teach others the song—

'The Night's seven eyes are fast asleep,
She's resting
On the dark moon
Turn away your eyes,
Tonight release us from your gaze,
Resting
On the dark moon
Don't paralyze us with your eyes,
We're escaping your seven eyes
From your silent tyranny—
No one knows
Why this night is not like the others,
Why this night is night for Night,

She sleeps—
While her bloody tresses bind the veins of heaven'

This last line being repeated throughout for a long interval it is pitched higher for each word—there are preparations—

The unknown priest who is not known for wearing the seven-eye mask brings the one who put himself forward for the night of the Night and who is not known for wearing the sacrifice's mask, there is no light but what comes from the idol and that is not light, that is not light that is coming out of the idol, but shines so they can see the masks, the priest lies on the couch and says—

'I sleep'

the one in the mask of the sacrifice comes up to the couch—except the priest they sing constantly—

'While her bloody tresses bind up the veins of heaven'

—the one in the mask of the sacrifice lies beside the priest and he is given the moon's sour opium to drink, and when he lies on the couch they send their voices invisible as shadows in shadow one voice to the sky and the stars past the sleeping Night whose jealousy is also asleep and does not run after their calls to hem them in below the arch of the moon—

The priest rises, the white gold knife of the priest writes the language of night on the body of the offering by whose blood as it comes they can see, until the dark moon disappears, the priest makes cuts and gives admittance to the night to the body of the offering, the offering will know the night in every part of himself, and while the unknown priest is cutting beneath the idol of moons the rest are safe and unseen to kiss in the dark and sing—

'Now they are all gaping diamond veins of heaven'

and the offering cries—

'Now my blood escaping shines through the gaze of heaven'

—in a voice that shakes the ground—the voice of the offering comes out of the offering and speaks in all of them, the voice of the offering disappears and for a moment there is nothing in the world, the night for All, there is night for All, and Nothing—

And those who return see the twilight again, by twilight in the east as the dark moon sets each takes a piece of the offering to hide in the earth before the sun shines.

The Death of Edgar Allan Poe

I had been called to the home of a dying friend, and waited on him. In my haste and confusion I had neglected to bring with me my hat or my coat, but had thoughtlessly, distractedly rushed out from my home into the street when I received the news—what a frenzy of wind! And yet no rain has fallen, but all the streets and their tributary lanes—normally so bright at this time of year, that even at night they showed a cheerful, inviting appearance—were deadened with a stationary pall of dismal cloud. The blast that met me in the street was a skein of warm and cold, its frenzied repulsion delayed my arrival at my friend's house, for I proceeded on foot.

But after some struggle with the elements, I turned into the narrow iron gate and trod the path to the front door of my friend's house. The lights in the windows were few and somber, and nearly engulfed in the prevailing gloom. The two tall Dutch doors were flanked by a pair of feeble lamps, whose gleams seemed dissipated by the tempest.

I knocked, and was presently admitted by my friend's man, to whom I made my necessarily breathless apologies. Although the house was extremely spacious, I was informed that my friend lay in the adjoining apartment to the foyer. As a number of his relations were with him at that time, and that these persons were, for reasons I did not fully understand, inimical to me, I was requested to wait in the foyer.

The servant retired to inform my friend of my arrival. In his absence I repeatedly traversed the small space of the foyer. I must now confide that I am a constitutionally excitable man. It is a curious thing, that my nerves are highly susceptible to perturbation only by a certain obscure species of stimuli, whose common, essential character remains a mystery to me. Tempestuous conditions, storms, lightnings, all manner of disruption in the weather, will be especially volatilizing to me. So, my friend's servant found me in a state of considerable agitation upon his return.

I was instructed to wait his master's sufferance, and an appropriate pause in his interview with his relations. He then expressed to me that he was fatigued, having been all day occupied in tending to my friend, and inquired of me permission to sit down. I replied in the affirmative, and continued to traverse the floor. The veillety of my friend's servant only made me the more powerfully aware of my own extreme excitation, which seemed rather to be mounting than subsiding, although I had been within doors for many minutes. In my growing exuberance I felt a bounding vitality, which, had I been admitted at once into the company of my dying friend, would have been a shocking and impious impropriety. And yet it did not subside. The foyer was brilliantly illuminated by a glinting crystal lamp, whose dazzling light was another irritant. Soon I found it difficult to contain myself, I paced rapidly, and made small, furtive gestures with my hands, half-dreading with each step that I should suddenly find myself unable to control my limbs.

And outside the thin walls of my friend's house, the wind bellowed and battered like a mad thing! I admit that a peculiar fancy took hold of me then. I thought that the wind was death, the death of my friend, terribly visiting this proud house to bear him away, and overtaken in an instant by a sort of delirium, I flung open the upper panel of one of the Dutch doors, and cried, "This flimsy wood will never keep it out!"

My friend's man hastened to refasten the door. I meanwhile strode forward, toward the hallway, which ran in either direction, to the right and to the left, in parallel with the door. However, my attention was arrested then by a small case, no larger than my palm, set into the wall of the foyer. On closer inspection, I saw that it housed a vertical row of buttons, adjacent to each of which there was a rectangular panel bearing a paper label, and adjacent to each of these, a tiny bulb. The labels named the various chambers in my friend's house, and, I assumed, that when a button was pushed, the occupants of the apartment named on the adjacent panel would be alerted in some manner. But among these labels, inscribed "kitchen", "parlor", "library", etc., there was one anomalous panel, that read "duel to the death".

I at once pressed the adjacent button, and watched as the bulb palely winked, and I at once, in my mind's eye, saw myself lying dead upon the floor of a room just up the hall. I knew this, beyond doubt, would come to pass, tonight, nearly immediately—and, in fact, had known it when, with a wild ebullience, I had pressed the button!

And yet, in my exalted state of provoked excitement, I experienced no fear, not the slightest trepidation, no horror of the death that, I was certain, would extinguish me within the hour. I seemed to look down upon myself from a sublime altitude, beyond reach of any suffering, elevated above fear, with no thought for my well being, or even my continued existence.

At this time, I was called into the presence of my friend. He lay upon a narrow bed, set endwise against the wall. The room was thoroughly, even over-brightly, illuminated. My friend's relatives stood separately or in pairs in various stations in the apartment, and none looked at me. I crossed to my friend's bedside almost in an instant, so buoyant was I that my step seemed to span the floor.

I sat beside him and laid my hand upon his brow. His face, though disheveled, was still fleshy, and exhibited no trace of pain or terror, no anguish, but only a calm, even a childishly placid, appearance. He smiled up at me with sparkling eyes, clasping the covers to his bosom.

I urged him not to speak, whereupon one of his relatives, a woman, who had been nursing him, replied with great acrimony, that he had not lost the power of speech. With perfect aplomb I rejoined to her merely that he did not have to speak to me, as my intuited understanding of his meaning look was total. He lay content, and at his ease, because he knew no threat of death, nor was he in danger of ceasing to live. He would lie there beneath the covers for perhaps a thousand years or more, perhaps, indeed, forever, satisfied, and complaisantly beyond the reach of mortality.

"I," I said, standing, "however, have an appointment to keep!" Whereupon, I quit the room, with the same telescopic ease and rapidity with which I had entered it, leaving my friend's relations thunderstruck, dumbfounded.

I strode down the hall, toward the room my vision had shown me. As I walked, I felt I took the great triumphal procession of my life's accomplishments. I bore with me, without effort, my entire past history, each moment, every thought, every impression, compassed in my mind, and felt as I walked that I bore myself toward my final consummation, that, as did the Attic heroes, I knew my fate, and strived to embrace it. The episodes of my life unfolded before me in sequence, and they appeared beautiful to me as never before. Never before was this life so precious or so exquisitely beautiful to me, as it was when I carried it entire to its destruction!

I opened a door, and found the room already aglow with many lanterns. It was a modest study. A piano stood by the draped window. A mirror, with a gilded frame, hung above a marble hearth. The walls were covered with crimson paper, and a thick black rug, spangled with snow-white blossoms, like stars in the firmament, was spread upon the floor. There was a small, round-topped wooden table before the door, and several vials of various drugs stood atop it. From these, I selected a black, cubical vial. I briefly glanced in the mirror, and saw there reflected my glinting eyes. I then uncorked the black vial, and drank its contents to the drains.

I stood before the mirror, and now, I from time to time look up from my writing, to the room through the golden frame, at the form that lies prostrate on the black rug.

Translation.

When Bob Price was still editing books for Chaosium, he planned a second anthology of Nyarlathotep stories, and invited me to contribute. As usual, the book was painstakingly assembled and never published. This story makes mention of Waghdas (here spelled with a U) from *Cities of the Red Night* by William S. Burroughs, a favorite among favorites, in an attempt to build a little bridge between the two sets of myths. Fans of Arthur Machen will make note of the "phoors" (voors).

Translation

In those anticipated days the Village was quiet, its streets were dim, the buildings that lined them were half-empty, where in an occasional window one might spot someone briefly parting black curtains, holding up a weak candle that would only feebly illuminate a face creased by anxiety, a thin lip of folded fabric where the curtain was held open, and no light streaming past from the invisible room. There was no sound of traffic, no sirens, horns, crowd noise, music, no man-made sound. Apart from your own footsteps, the coming and going of your breath, you would hear nothing but the wind folding around you like a parted curtain, and the sound of the air sliding through the trees. On the avenues, every now and then, a car did rush past, running the intersections, all the stoplights have been turned off, its headlights almost always turned off. In a so-far snowless December, the streets were completely derelict, except for the many feral cats that filled the city, most of them larger than usual, but harmless—they went everywhere, congregated silently, watched everything luminously. Also there were a great number of wild dogs in small packs; indigenous to the city, they had taken on their own traits of breed, more colorful than country dogs, more varied in appearance but generally favoring the lean, needle-headed variety. Most had no tongues, their mouths opened only slightly, at the front of their heads, and their teeth grew out the sides through their dewlaps, and through this modified mouth they would suck up steam from manholes, their only food. They would glide up and down each street in succession, in pairs or threesomes, completely silent, with wide saucerlike eyes, their heads veering regularly right and left.

On the sidewalk, only very rarely would you glimpse a half-imaginary walker, in the distance, or retracting into a doorway, where reflections of the dim streetlights would momentarily slide across the varnished surface of an otherwise invisible shutting door. In those days, one knocked at the doors of restaurants, and was admitted only after an up-and-down glance tossed from a high peephole. This glance was especially brief for X, here called Theodore, who was a regular at the E & C, which was like the inside of a wooden box, filled with small tables, each one lit with a tiny candle in a glass, the only light. He would sit by the window in an alcove and when the waitress would come and speak, her quiet voice would set the air ringing, because everyone else was quiet, and there were very few people. Theodore and the waitress would eye each other timidly, and, to spare their voices, or rather to spare the quiet, he would point out dishes on the menu, and she would nod, and then there would be no sound but the rasping of her pencil. The other diners, all sitting alone, kept their eyes down and ate furtively. When his food came, Theodore did the same.

Recently, Theodore had received word from Y, here called Eleanor, about a project. Eleanor had been working at the Jefferson Market Library, had suffered to see her job eliminated by the city, reducing the staff to one arthritic librarian. Eleanor nearly starved, there was no work. Now, in a letter lying whitely on the small table inserted between him and the sideboard, she wrote to Theodore of a translation project, she was required to select a partner, was he interested? Theodore, who had recently lost his job when the school collapsed, was on his way to see her, to accept the work eagerly. When he left the restaurant, the wind blew out his coat, the door locked behind him, the two gestures clockworkly linked.

Eleanor lived in a short alley, blocked at the far end by the sluggish overflow of the Hudson, half-clotted and eddying in mud and old rubbish across the concrete platform of West avenue. The wind flued past her recessed door in transparent blue streaks, sucked hysterically cold by the water over which it had passed, over which it was passing. At present, Theodore stepped to the still cobbled lane, with its margin of dirt sprouting dingy trees to one side. Eleanor lived at #12, a two-story brick face covered over with dirty-white plaster. All along the lane, one illuminated window shed its light in dark space like a sonar ping, Eleanor's upstairs room. Theodore knocked and waited, the wind blasting him continuously, hardening his face and hands and making the flesh brittle and clear. The door was heavy, with a knocker but no handle and two keyholes, one on the side, one in the center. They both jostled and made a dull thud each, then the door opened and Eleanor waved him quickly inside.

They jammed together in the tiny aperture at the foot of the stairs, Theodore fumbling off his heavy coat with her faltering help, while the city loomed as empty as a desert for miles in every direction around them. The upstairs rooms were filled with smoke from a clogged flue and Eleanor tore holes in the cloud with her heavily-bangled hands. She and Theodore were exactly the same age, and both Egyptologists, now more than ever before a subject with limitless horizons. Enormous federal budgets poured into frantic digs in the Sahara, new discoveries sluiced in every day, but competition was fierce and neither Theodore nor Eleanor had experience on-site, so they stayed at home and starved. They were free enough in each other's presence to be informally businesslike and candid; Theodore nakedly wanted to skip the formalities and get to work.

Eleanor brought Theodore immediately over to her desk, which filled half the room, which was not a small room, and introduced Theodore to a dozen neat piles of papers, explaining as she pulled up her stockings, "Steiniz uncovered this at Avaris—it's a Demotic translation of the *Book of Nephren-Ka*."

[This Ninth Dynasty text, written by the Pharaoh Nephren-Ka himself in either an unknown language or a private cipher, has remained untranslated.] Eleanor said, "No corresponding hieroglyphic translation of the *Book* was found, and this Demotic translation has only made things more confusing. The characters and vocabulary transpose for the most part, but the grammar is still incomprehensible. So my employer wants us to do two things—first, to determine if this Demotic translation is genuine, and if so, to reverse-engineer the grammar from comparison with the Demotic."

The pages she indicated, with a few rigorous and self-confident gestures, were high-resolution copies of the original scroll, shadowy edges crumbling in outline against the crisp borders of the print-out pages, still totally legible. The body of the text was completely intact and filled eleven sheets, in small script, laid out in unusually perfect rows and columns.

"We should translate this into hieroglyphics first," Theodore said. Eleanor had already started—she showed him her sketchy results.

"There are no independent characters. Everything here is integral, so we can only go so far working word-by-word. Our translation will depend on whether or not we can get a sense of a pattern, then we'll have to combine all the elements in conformity with that pattern before any of it will take on sense."

They sat down together, and Theodore watched Eleanor's hair sweep gradually down from her shoulders strand by strand, hang vertically on either side of her face, waft finely in the warm draughts from the hearth, gleam a little with platinum gleams. Her bangs were fine and short and burlesquely arched to either side of the top of her forehead like a golden upper lip. He certainly noticed Eleanor closely. Her demeanor called up in him a coordinated clarity as he swept his gaze unchanged from her to the text.

They worked together, excitedly trying one tactic after another, even-tempered and unfrustrated but making little progress, until the sun came up. Theodore brought some things from his apartment and they ate sandwiches together. He slept at the foot of her bed, rolled on the floor in a blanket.

Without relenting they kept at the manuscript, showing no sign of strain and not getting bored, but the pattern that emerged came out in them, not in the translation. Having somehow divined from the first that the sense of the writing was spatial, he would establish regular grammatical clusters by means of small grids, and she would fill in the proper characters. Once he had isolated all the smaller clusters, he went to work grouping them into larger knots, and she filled out the contours as he drew them. At the end of the week they had organized the writing enough for Eleanor to decide that the Demotic was most likely a genuine translation, although an undeciphered one. She sent a letter to her employer, and some ration stamps and even a little paper money came back in the mail. Eleanor grinned and held out her palm, clicked her nails, coaxed out a handful of tokens from the rigid envelope, blue for sugar, red for meat.

Theodore took his afternoon walk that day, just before nightfall, along the river. He came back limping—bitten by a dog. The wound was small and deeply painful, but healed quickly. He and Eleanor stared at each other in silence, when he showed her. He could not afford rabies shots.

She commiserated with him a moment, and brewed him some milk steamed with tea—there was no coffee—before going back to review their results. Theodore washed his leg in the kitchen sink. When he rejoined her, Eleanor was bent nearly double over the desk and writing quickly. At a pause she waved the sleeves of her kimono at him, her eyes bright, saying, "I think the characters are grouped by number!"

Looking at her, the flush of her face became a brilliant cloud in which Theodore lost the next few days, overflowing them with intense work at the translation, as if it had sucked him in through her face. No fever developed, and Theodore forgot about the bite without noticing it. Incredibly alert, he and she both, filled with sharp and eager understanding, chafingly fitting and refitting characters, they worked numbered groupings at various orders, they turned avid attention increasingly to the arrangement of the glyphs in connected clustered strings, and days were spinning recklessly by unheeded outside the window when Theodore realized all at once, entirely, that the book was constructed in phases, such that one wave of grammatical morphology was superimposed upon another, making the text more dense than long. The entire book was a single passage which was to be read repeatedly in a predetermined sequence of grammatical modes and fully understood only at the last. The passage had to be read either over and over, using a different grammar each time (in the right evolutionary order), or simultaneously in all the grammars used, at once. When this unfolded in front of him, the page seemed to blossom out and enravel him, he could see that the grammar was not only symmetrical within each line, as a one-dimensional figure, but symmetrical for all characters on the page and in the book considered as an unfolded whole sheet like a multi-symmetrical two-dimensional figure—and when he understood that, he understood that the grammar was also supersymmetrical, in that each element was balanced in each different grammatical reading, that when all readings were layered one atop another in the right order, it would harmonize like a supersymmetrical object in three dimensions—and when he understood that, he saw the entire text unfold in front of him in calculine symmetry as a single statement, a single word, a single name, and he felt his spirit being ravished half out of himself, to see such unanthropic order so impossible to grasp but close enough to intelligibility to flicker as intangibly as fire on his nerves, a fire-faceted blossom in a shadowy spot just beyond possible reach, but nevertheless real and meaningful, a word written by a man blind and insane; to think of it all at once he felt pure abstract flavorless pleasure drain into him down his long nerves, feeling beautiful, anonymous, fainting back into a soft little aperture of pleasure in space, a sort of pain as if his soul were being gradually licked out of his heart in slow slow wonderful ebbs—deep satisfaction, just to have been given to understand that much, just to glimpse the problem clearly for once, a breakthrough in his mind that hummed real physical pleasure down in slow shivers into his cells, next to his nerves. And when he called to Eleanor, he felt his heart quicken, and when she looked up, he looked only at her face and especially her eyes, and when she finally came over and he showed her what he meant on the page, he watched her face, he watched her and watched her with his hands shaking and his heart rattling, also his breathing going faster and shallower, and then she saw it, it all unfolded for her just as it had for him; she all at once and entirely grasped the supersymmetry of the grammar, and confirmed it, and he could see with mental ecstasy that she was nearly swooned, she beamed and she looked up to the ceiling and patted her face, ran her fingers through her hair, thoroughly rapt in the inspiration of that total order. The sun was up by that time and was filling the room from the windows. With a voice that slid under the sunlight and at the same time chimed with pleasure she purred, "Yes … it's all total clarity to every horizon, on every level."

Together dream-drunk with the ready potentiality of that single name, brought within reach by a single organic insight, they began training their bodies to read it. Over the weekend, after a day lost to satisfied daydreaming in bland auburn sunlight, sitting together a little stunned and all at once out of practice with work, they resumed the project on Monday as if only just naturally discovering a mutual aptitude for it. They immediately began itemizing the name's grammatical elements on stacks of index cards, then sat, with their knees touching, swapping the cards back and forth, trying to assemble them in order, finding ways to reduce and homogenize them—even translated, the heterogeneous elements had to be fully homogenized—working with fewer and fewer cards as each steadily collapsed into each. They worked and collapsed into each other, so that, when he fell back in exhaustion, she fell back in exhaustion. The pace of collation slowed at regular intervals until they deadlocked at eight cards. These eight passed unceasingly back and forth for two days with no progress, until Eleanor broke free, drained. She undressed and rested.

Although he was weak, Theodore couldn't rest. He ended up on the street. The neighborhood was now entirely unfamiliar to him—at first, he hadn't walked too fast, looking anxiously around at the buildings, but as he continued to fail to recognize them he turned his eyes to the ground and quickened his pace; he realized he was afraid. His head felt soft, he put his hands to his head, when he could find his head—asking himself, what's wrong with who? Who is here? He looked back to find he had disappeared, he was watching himself not being there, where he had always been before—suddenly the panicky idea that he had never been there, that he had only ever been the fear in this one moment, happening to no one and wholly confined to itself. He looked at his body with surprise, and felt it, and then with relief he seized hold of it and calmed himself. His body had not changed, but he felt it differently, he was directly conscious of the ghostly life that was there in each smallest part. He tried to calm himself, standing absentmindedly on a deserted street corner, stilling himself with listening attention, trying at the same time to trace the new impressions back to the source, the new sense he was just now feeling. He felt himself directly connected with the weather, the ground, the light coming from the sun—he was all of a sudden aware of being only partially separate from them; this wasn't an idea, it was an exhilarating intuition. Now he knew he was crouching down beside a front stoop, staring at a planter directly in front of him. The tree that had been there was long uprooted for firewood, but there were a few tender shoots, even now, kept from freezing by a steam grate in the street, that were alive and growing there. Theodore could see, directly, the life that was in them, and he ate them, to feel them still alive in his mouth as he chewed, and to feel that life reorganize itself inside him as it merged with his own. The green breath of that life released him a while later at the foot of Eleanor's bed, and he collapsed there, senseless.

That night, like sleepwalkers, they rose together and feverishly began work again. The manuscript and the index cards were the first things and only things they saw. The name would not emerge gradually—they would have to have all the parts ready, and they would come together at once, in the one proper fashion, only then. Theodore worked until his head fell forward onto the table, out cold. Eleanor blinked up at weird-looking sunlight glancing in through the window, then impulsively stepped outside. She surprised a dog in the alley—it snarled, and then viciously snapped at her. Eleanor whipped a rock in its direction and unexpectedly struck its head; the dog staggered two steps sideways and dropped to the ground.

Without thinking, she went over to it, breathless, excited. The dog wasn't bleeding, but its head wobbled on its neck, dazed; something winked on in Eleanor as she looked at it. She saw its life directly, without needing any secondary motion of thought, but simply, like a color. Without seeing, feeling, or hearing it, without using any proper sense, she perceived it somehow and was fascinated. Even in this stray dog it was complicated, synchronized, elaborate, symmetrical. The dog recovered itself and stood up, barking explosively, cornered against the wall. The noise and sudden motion clanged against Eleanor's nerves and she stumbled back a little from where she had knelt. The dog barked and put its ears back. Eleanor somehow knew how active it was inside, but all the racket was too distracting. She had put her hand on another stone when she fell back, and now cracked the dog's head with it. The dog crumpled, pewling. Eleanor had only struck it a glancing blow and knelt over it, planting the rock solidly so that the impact jarred her arm, and a little blood came out onto the pavement. She could see it was still alive, then—her racing heart, her rapid, shallow breath—all at once opened out and down into herself that same sense, minute and precious chemistry in every part of her, orchestrated, living things arranged in symmetrical levels from cells to tissues to organs to organ systems and then to an organism, and now there was an appetite in her to extend further her own organism with another. Eleanor fetched a knife from the kitchen and cut the dog's throat, intuitively knowing where to cut, and caught the blood in a bowl she had brought, draining it every time it filled, delighted to feel the living blood in her mouth and inside her, merging its life with hers, its red breath simmering dry thermals in her brain like alcohol.

And later, when she came inside, Theodore was awake, sitting with the index cards. She put away the knife and bowl and cleaned her face, then stood in the doorway, unnoticed, and watched his cool, white, dry hands flash, gleaming like knives, through the air at the ends of his black cuffs, where these cuffs were cinched at the wrist, so that none of the arm showed. Yes she watched him and certainly she felt it too, loved him—she saw something there that shocked her: she saw the name taking shape in him, partially, and realized by reflection that the name was taking shape in her, writing itself with their life. Nearly ecstatic, Eleanor understood the fathomless complexity of the life she was looking at, and now her other appetite was whetted, she wanted to join her life with his, and especially it struck her that she must experience pregnancy in this condition, what would it be like to feel so acutely the little shift that would start in her, then that internal extension of her own life growing and elaborating itself inexorably every day. Eleanor came into the room and, with her hand, she turned his head. With a start she clearly felt him inside touch her naked life in his mind. She brought him into her arms and to the bed without speaking and each of them fed back consciousness and pleasure.

*

Then announcements break through the wireless—severe weather conditions immanent, a year-long blizzard on the way, the governor has signed an immediate evacuation order. Theodore and Eleanor stare at each other in panic and confusion, then start frantically packing up the manuscript, the notes, the cards.

"How much gas is there?"

"A gallon or two—enough to drop by your place and pick up a few things if you want. We should get to the phone first."

There are two working phones at the post office. After an hour in line, with more panicking citizens trailing in minute by minute, Theodore books a too-expensive flight to Los Angeles.

"I still have the keys to my cousin's house."

They make the bridge before the rush—the tunnels had begun leaking years ago and were by now knee-deep and impassable—dodging broken cables drooping over the lanes. Brooklyn flashes in their windows, overrun by trees.

Presently, the broken-jawed jumble of derelict buildings and hangars at JFK, bright orange signs with spray-stenciled directions to the one operating terminal. Eleanor beaches her car on the sidewalk at the loading zone, and they run together into the half-dark, draughty terminal. They check in at the gate.

Long delays on into the early morning. The floor is filling, knots of people in tiny patches of light, huddling together for warmth, shivered by icy gusts threading through them from the cracked, wall-sized windows. Outside, the runways and taxiways are littered with drooping and semi-collapsed aircraft, a few prop planes are taking off from time to time. Then around sunrise a converted cargo plane rumbles up to the window and a steward appears at the gate with two armed security guards, calling for tickets over the earsplitting droning of the engines, ushering passengers onto the tarmac, turning away the stand-bys. Theodore and Eleanor hold their breath, pass the gate, and board, blowing steam and rubbing their hands as they file up the stairway. Moments later, the pilot slams the hatch behind them and rushes forward to the cockpit. The plane turns from the gate and threads its way through the hulks, the shadowy runway lit with free-standing lanterns, torches, and burning tires. Now a lurch forward at speed and with three brief jerks they're rising fast, then circling back over the airport—as they turn the sun appears behind them, its rays reflected back toward the horizon by a black hood of clouds closing in from the north.

The flight is full, but now the people are calm. Theodore and Eleanor have seats set off a bit from the rest, bolted down toward the back of the plane, where the windows are. They sit with their knees angled toward each other, swapping cards. They tick the six that are left back and forth from hand and eye to hand and eye, and below them the land changes from green to brown, now the earth is cryptically marked in sparse places, less obviously so many towns and roads, lights, sublimating into streaks and points at this middle altitude, and rarefying, the details of the landscape are less definite, each one has its own amorphous, isolating margin of empty country, these margins become clearer than the details over time and expand to form measureless gaps bordered by the horizon—the plane seems to be vibrating in space clear to every horizon above the ground.

In the hours that follow, Theodore and Eleanor trade their index cards, reducing their number faster and faster, and with rising excitement to feel the Pacific rolling over the curvature of the earth, momentarily nearer to them, so that if they kept going, the brown field underneath would give way to chaotic blue-green frothed with white, seeming far vaster than dry land. Without announcement, the plane suddenly dips forward, peeling off momentum and altitude; they are circling down, sliding off slopes of air mounded up atop the mountains. The city appearing beneath them is clear and full of very bright sunlight—an untended fire sends an unwavering column of smoke straight up, and they descend through it at high altitude, sweeping down parallel to the coast. Eleanor has the window seat; she can see a vast herd of leopards running up the beach below them as so many dodging spots and almost invisible patches of blonde fur racing over blonde sand. The plane drops as if it was sliding off the edge of a titanic bubble and the engines shake the plane as if they and the tidal force were rattling it apart—Theodore and Eleanor shut their eyes and take each other by the hand, and by this they take each other completely, and hang in suspense until the runway flashes up beneath them and the plane batters down the air onto it. In their clenched hands, their index cards are straight and uncrumpled. Even frightened, the two of them have become so vivid, they're irradiating the passengers, vibrating cancer down into their cells. In the next few weeks, they will all begin growing again, sprouting fabulous new structures, tubefeet, heatsinks, and erogenous feelers and glands budding and fleshing out with euphoric industry in the tissues. The children they have spirited safely away from the storm will grow up more dramatically than expected.

On the ground, the terminal is calm and deserted. Theodore and Eleanor rent a car and leave at once, moving in straight lines down a calm and deserted freeway, toward the foothills, the manuscript lying between them as an adulterous secret. Something is watching over them like a jealous spouse, an angry parent, something that is also taking shape in them both—both taking shape in them and giving them shape, impatiently changing a shape given them long ago.

*

Theodore and Eleanor at the house: in a deserted neighborhood, in an empty canyon—coming to the house finally, their one and only place to go, it's where they've been heading together from the start, they'll go no farther, they both understand this intuitively as they sit in the car, watch the house appear at the end of the street. The wind is strongly blowing; the whole canyon is stirring.

Each the same can see clearly to the short time ahead, free if only to work and be changed some more, but the future has become decisive, with a

93

definite direction and the word of their work at the end. Dried leaves, curled in on themselves like seashells, scrape up the drive before them on the wind as they come from the car together. The house is modest and plain, with a concrete porch. Inside, they will find some sticks of furniture, bare plaster walls perforated in places with painted-over nails, running water and electricity, a small store of canned food on the shelves in the pantry, a few boxes of books-paper-pens-paper clips and so on, one bed. With the wind rushing by outside, the low air turning pink as the sun sets across from them on the horizon, the hills embracing them are green and brown, the sky is perfect azure and clear—inside the house the light from the windows will intermittently dim down, amid shimmering shadows of leaves from the oaks growing all around to twice the height of Theodore's cousin's house, this shimmering light will suddenly die down, be dim for a few minutes, and then grow strong again; the light is synchronized with each new gust of wind, which hisses along the walls of the house. Together they move a table up against the wall, between and level with two windows, bring in a small lamp, set out the remaining cards, the manuscript in the middle on a writing desk. They sit beside each other, happy to be here, safely out of the way, where the work can be pursued to its end.

Here, the silence, the embrace of each other's presence, above that the embrace of the house, the scores of empty and embalmed houses hovering dreamlike on all sides, then the web of trees, then the hills all around, the wind, then the chrysalis of the sky and infinite distance, set them all the more calmly, and with a sense of inevitability, to the task. They slept and ate in modest turns. In a trance they now traded three index cards back and forth, in full view of their hieroglyphic translation and the Demotic copy laid side by side.

For a full day they mechanically stared at the three cards remaining, like dummies beside each other, like two translations from the same source laid side by side. Then at once they keyed the third card to the first, and were left with two. Coyotes were yipping under the streetlight outside. Their tightly-knotted pack burst apart as it happened, sending flashing streams of coyotes in all directions—a few insinuated themselves around the house, going swiftly by to the dark hillside on blinking feet, in columns of softly panting shadows.

The next morning, they woke to discover that a letter of congratulations had come, from Eleanor's employer, along with two tins of food. They ate hastily, with nothing to say to each other, and returned as quickly as possible to staring at the two cards that remained, that would combine in one name that they would both speak, with which they were both pregnant. Eleanor sat, flicking her eyes madly from one to the other, too excited to concentrate, unable to see anything more than two words lying on the table, too excited even to be frustrated; and Theodore could only see his shaking hands lying bunched up in front of him. When these two elements were harmonized, he and Eleanor would have made the movement of translating for the last time, and the change he had long been expecting would be finished. As long as he thought about that change, he was overwhelmed by the effort of considering it, and too exhausted to move forward. The two index cards outlined between them a gap that would be filled when the translation was done, and, transfixed by it, he lost track of time. He was certain Eleanor was fascinated by the same space between the cards. They both wanted to prolong their contact with it as it was just at the threshold, because they wouldn't be the same after it appeared.

Then Theodore looked up and saw a buck staring in through the window, with a long needle-shaped head and a mouth that opened only at the very front, black animal alien eyes under weirdly spreading antlers. Theodore was caught instantly in its unmoving gaze and saw something in this animal's face like a living desert with a yawning, indifferent stare, like the sunlight, or open space, nothing he hadn't seen before, nothing he had ever noticed, seeing him, with indifference. He saw the buck was alive and seeing him clearly, and he acutely felt Eleanor beside him as she looked up and joined in the triangle of looking eyes. All at once the buck moved weightlessly off—having looked, it passively looked elsewhere and disappeared in a continuous outpouring of wind out of nowhere.

Eleanor had seen the buck's eyes and was shocked, looked down at the cards with a cauterized mind, and seized Theodore's hand as his eyes automatically dropped down to the cards and, with one motion coordinated for the last time in two bodies, they combined the cards with a few pen scratches and the name silently appeared, clicked through them as they spoke it in gelatinous waves on fixed and timeless air. The wind dropped, the light from the windows steadily dimmed, the cards shone white and winked out on the completely darkened table. As they combined the cards, Theodore and Eleanor slid together and overlapped with a click, and what had been gestating in them appeared in their place—each of them perceived this separately as a contraction of the room, the door flying violently open and something like a jealous spouse storming in and almost completely darkening the room forever, and as it came in for them, Eleanor, with Theodore inside her and vice-versa, said "My Employer!"

*

The Book

The original text dated from the Ninth Dynasty, adding Nephren-Ka's name to the other three pharaonic names known from that period. It was written by Nephren-Ka himself, in an unknown language, possibly a cipher of his own making. The book remained an uncracked mystery until Steiniz uncovered a Demotic copy of the book, with an appended history from a Ninth Dynasty scribe, presumably an eyewitness, translated from a lost hieroglyphic account, and reproduced below. The Demotic translation of the Nephren-Ka text, from the scribe's original hieroglyphic translation, also lost, proved only slightly less impenetrable than the original—while the characters and some of the vocabulary could be made out, the crypto-grammar continues to frustrate all attempts at rendering the *Book* intelligible.

The Scribe's History

Nephren-Ka was a beautiful child. Beloved of everyone and the best of hunters, he once killed a ten-foot crocodile.

When his older brother died, Nephren-Ka grieved. For days he stared into the desert and refused to see anyone.

When his father died, Nephren-Ka was made Pharaoh. He grieved for his father. The people rejoiced when Nephren-Ka became the Living   Sun [1]. His beautiful face gave them pleasure.

In the second year of his reign, Nephren-Ka grieved the death of his sister, who would have been his wife. All his family had died. Nephren-Ka stared into the desert and refused to see anyone. He watched jackals in the desert and would look without blinking into their faces.

At the end of the second year of his reign, Nephren-Ka saw the sun devoured [witnessed an eclipse]. Everywhere there was fear. Everyone was calling on Nephren-Ka. Nephren-Ka watched as the sun was devoured and he laughed, he gave his people no comfort. The sun returned and he was laughing, and the people saw that he had been blinded. At that time the people said that the Living Sun was blind and insane.

From that time Nephren-Ka [was] almost blind [could see only very dimly]. He watched the desert at night and during the day, and brought jackals and vultures into his house and watched them.

In the third year of his reign, Nephren-Ka received Niarat-Hotep [2] of Uaghdas, the City of Wisdom [3]. This was a young Prince of Uaghdas who was white as ivory and whose hair was white as ivory, and who had lips and eyes the color of rubies, and who wore no clothes. Niarat-Hotep was young and beautiful. He danced for Nephren-Ka. Wide-eyed, Nephren-Ka saw Niarat-Hotep dancing and laughed.

Nephren-Ka and Niarat-Hotep were always together. Niarat-Hotep danced for Nephren-Ka. Nephren-Ka laughed.

At the beginning of the fourth year of his reign, Nephren-Ka began to make wars.

At that time, Nephren-Ka told the priests that the Living Sun was red and could see only red. The priests brought him a thousand slaves and he told the priests to kill the slaves and to allow their heart's blood to cover everything, so that he could see. The people said that the Living Sun was blind and insane.

The land was blighted. The Nile sank into the ground. Everyone starved and died in plagues.

Nephren-Ka stayed with Niarat-Hotep. At that time, he made many wars and captured thirty-thousand slaves. The people ate the slaves. The people withered and became strange, and ate corpses. No one was starving. With my own eyes I saw them do this. There was no one in the road who was not eating dead and living people. I saw dead people walking in the road.

Nephren-Ka stayed with Niarat-Hotep.

When I saw this, the morning was always red, the sky was red and stinking, the ground was red and steaming. There was no food or water but carrion and blood. Everywhere there were dead bodies and blood running on the ground. There were fires in the dried fields, and in the towns. The people burned and were eaten. The smoke covered the sun. The ground was black with flies. The people ate with the flies. I saw them pursue dead people without heads running into the desert, and rotting and dead corpses ran from them and were caught and eaten. Nephren-Ka and Niarat-Hotep were eating their slaves.

The people became strange/not people. I saw this with my own eyes. This is how the ghouls [4] were made.

Acagchemem was in the desert. He was one of the generals of Nephren-Ka. When he returned to the land, the ghouls attacked his army and killed a number of soldiers. He took his army back into the wilderness. He swore an oath to kill Nephren-Ka. I saw this with my own eyes. With the great Scribe [5], my teacher, I fled to be with Acagchemem in the wilderness.

In the wilderness, the Scribe made a phoor [6] against Nephren-Ka. He drew an eye in stone and made a phoor. I saw this.

This was the beginning of the fifth year of the reign of Nephren-Ka.

Acagchemem went to war on Nephren-Ka. The Scribe made a phoor and the ghouls were all killed by the army of Acagchemem.

The ghouls all died or fled into the desert, or were also chased into the ocean, by Acagchemem and the armies of Acagchemem.

Acagchemem called Nephren-Ka out of his palace. Nephren-Ka was laughing. Acagchemem wrestled with Nephren-Ka for three days. After three days, Nephren-Ka was strangled.

Acagchemem went to find Niarat-Hotep. Niarat-Hotep had fled. Acagchemem died. His body was covered with incisions that stank of poison. When his body was washed he no longer stank. He was buried in a mastaba and an eye was carved by the Scribe in stone where he lay. The Scribe said all tombs must have this eye against the ghouls.

The lieutenant of Acagchemem, who was also his brother, told the priests to burn Nephren-Ka. One of the priests went mad when Nephren-Ka spoke as he was burned. The priests told the brother of Acagchemem that Nephren-Ka had spoken as he burned, and the brother of Acagchemem told the priests to cut Nephren-Ka apart and to grind his pieces to dust and destroy them, and to disperse the dust in the desert, and they did this.

The brother of Acagchemem was made Pharaoh. The good people came out from where they were hiding. He told them to take down the house of Nephren-Ka and bury the stones in the desert, and they did this. The land was restored.

(1) This designation was apparently unique to Nephren-Ka's reign.

(2) A proper name in a khartouche; one of the letters used is not identifiable, i.e. Niar*at-Hotep, possibly a foreign letter.

(3) It is not known to what city this refers.

(4) Word of uncertain origin. "Ghoul" is a substitution, from the Arabic word *ghul*, meaning ghost.

(5) The Scribe's identity is not known.

(6) A literal translation of an unknown word. There is no indication, other than the textual, of its meaning.

The Water Nymphs.

This is one of my first Lovecraftian stories. The gigantic blue vampire cadaver buried beneath "The Shunned House" has always struck me as one of his most bizarre and dreamlike images, and I wanted to get to know them, or at least their parasites, better.

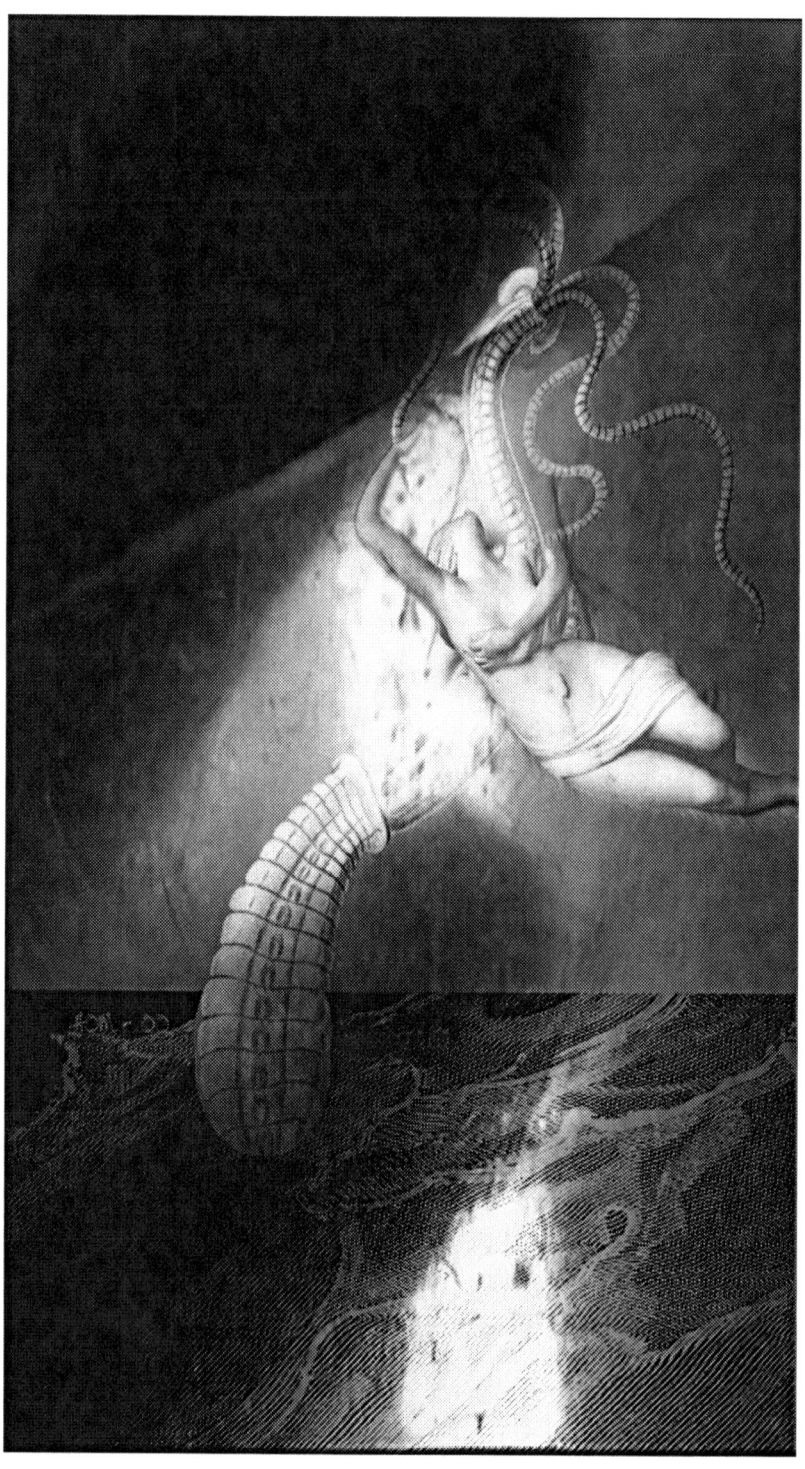

The Water Nymphs

My uncle William died a number of years ago, and what little he left behind was sold to pay his debts. His daughter summarily decided that the few sad boxes of unsellable rubbish that remained would be stored in my basement. She confidently lied to me, promising to take them off my hands when she got a bigger place. Several months later, bored, wandering at random through my empty house, I went down to the basement to sort through his things—this was the first time it ever occurred to me to be curious about them. After rummaging through his papers for a few moments, I began to get a growing sense of his rather plain, uninteresting life. His letters would have been too dull to read if it hadn't been for an arresting quality in the writing itself—the content of his letters was thoroughly ordinary, but I sensed an unusually lively and unhappy mind in his style. I began hunting for more personal articles of his, piecing together as I did so a sense of presence, my uncle's presence, mating it as best I could to the sparse childhood memories I had of him. I was delighted to find an old diary in among his things.

It had been bound shut with a heavy piece of twine. The knot had been sealed with wax, and, looking at it more closely, I could see an X impression in the seal. From the chafing on the binding and the brittleness of the twine, it seemed the diary had been sealed for a long time, very probably for years before my uncle's death. The twine and the seal disturbed me. It seemed to make this more than a family secret. For the same reason, I had no choice but to cut the twine and read.

The first half was just like his letters, although clearly the work of a younger and more hopeful man, and of no special interest. I have edited the second half into this narrative:

From the diary of William Slaite [entries are not dated]

Dr. Hilton called this morning, to say that mother is much worse. I've made arrangements to go up to Portland tomorrow—in the meantime, the idea that I may lose her is so painful that I have to struggle to drive those thoughts from my mind in order to go on. I understand that Miriam is there with her, and I occupy myself thinking of reunion with her. She was only thirteen or fourteen the last time we saw each other—all this time she has been away, I suddenly find that I miss her. In hindsight I wonder if I ever stopped thinking of her for a moment since. I've heard so little about her—I think she just got married.

[Miriam was his sister. They were not raised together—she was born after he was sent away to boarding school, and he saw her only intermittently.]

[Arriving in Portland] I made straight for the hospital from the train station and found mother and Miriam together. They both looked up at me as I came into the room with my bag under my arm, and I saw that the color had returned to mother's face, and that Miriam seemed relaxed and content. They were delighted to see me. Miriam took me aside and explained that mother had taken a bad turn earlier, but was now improving rapidly.

She said, "You've come all this way for nothing!"

I told her that was nonsense.

We weren't raised together, and every time we saw each other we met each other for the first time. When I look at Miriam now, it's as if I'm gazing into an enchanted mirror, seeing a female version of myself. I sense our common life. Miriam is beautiful. I'm afraid I "melted all over her"! We spent every moment together, leaving mother when she had to sleep. Dr. Hilton assured us she was recovering, and insisted that we get out of the hospital for a while. I walked Miriam back to her hotel. Neither of us had much appetite. I couldn't take my eyes off of her. I love Miriam. I watched her go back into her hotel. She prefers dresses made of very stiff material, and I could hear her skirts rustling as she went inside. I walked back to my hotel, and I felt her walking alongside me. She was with me from that moment on, every moment.

Her features are exceedingly sharp, but the expanse of her narrow face is as soft as the billow of a sail. I see her face before me all the time.

Today I met her for breakfast. She had arrived first—her table was reserved under the name "Mrs. Herman". I asked about her husband, and she smiled at me, a little faintly I thought. She said that his first name was Elie, they'd met in school, and that he's a folklorist. At the moment he's working on a book of Penobscot legends, collecting stories in the woods in an extremely remote town called Sloan.

She said "It's really only a handful of old houses, with a church and a general store."

A dirt road is the only link with the rest of the world. Apparently she lives with him out there, in the middle of nowhere. I didn't say anything, but I suppose she was accustomed to explain—"We'll only be there until Elie finishes his notes, in a few months." She's very matter-of-fact about it, but I wonder how happy she really is.

Now, as I think over what she said, I feel frightened for her. My throat feels as if it's been clamped shut. I wish she wouldn't go back, but would stay here in Portland with mother. I wish mother wasn't improving so quickly, to keep her here. I'll stay as long as she stays. I want to go with her, or keep her here, or bring her back with me.

[My uncle's mother, Eleanor Slaite, made a full recovery in a few days, and, despite his protests, Miriam returned to Sloan. My uncle returned home to Boston shortly thereafter, and appears to have suffered terribly from missing his sister—their correspondence was slow, owing to the remoteness of Sloan.

[A little under four months after this meeting, Elie and Miriam left Sloan to return to Portland. A mail truck driver came across their car lying in a gully by the side of the road the morning after they left. There had been heavy rain for several nights in a row, and apparently they had taken a turn too hard and slid off the road. Elie and Miriam were thrown through the windshield. Their bodies were found lying close by each other, on the rocks. With more bad weather on the way, it was decided that the bodies should be brought back to Sloan. Word was sent to Eleanor Slaite, and she gave permission for their bodies to be buried there.]

Miriam is dead

I knew she was wrong to go back but she refused to listen to me.

I told you, Miriam, why you shouldn't go.

I love you more than I love my own life, why should I have lied to you? How could I?

I offered her as much of my life as she wanted, she could stay here with me and I would have looked after her better than anyone.

I love you better than anyone else could.

I never had you and now I've lost you.

Miriam is dead is all I say to myself all day—every waking moment I tell myself you are dead.

Your face is always before me.

[Shortly after this was written, my uncle checked himself into a hospital and was "diagnosed" with "nervous exhaustion". During this time he apparently either wrote nothing, or his writings were lost—the diary goes into hiatus for what appears to be an extended period, and then resumes on a wholly ordinary note. It appears that my uncle was trying to avoid writing or thinking about my aunt Miriam. Here is the first entry in which she is named again]:

When she [his mother] had gone, I started going through her things, deliberately. I knew there were items that Miriam had left that she was keeping back from me, afraid to show me. I was afraid, too.

I found a box of things in her closet, and I could tell that mother had been going through them, crying over them, and I felt my eyes burning. I dug through the stuff quickly, shouting myself down as I did, and suddenly I pawed up a small notebook with a hasp. When I opened it I recognized my sister's handwriting ... [original ellipsis]

[My uncle took her diary (which apparently no longer exists) and said nothing to his mother. He mentions reading it in a number of subsequent entries. His own diary becomes somewhat sparse and cryptic at this point, but at some point he decides to go to Sloan]:

I'm going to retrace her there.

On the train [en route to Fairvale, the nearest train stop to Sloan]—
Writing like Miriam—
motionless black water in among the grey leafless trees and the sun directly opposite me on the horizon, golden eye among the trees running alongside the train through the tree trunks
   leprous ponds still half covered in ice
   bleak marshy clearings
   brooks among the roots like snail-tracks against the sky the landscape streams unevenly by like black smoke—a few houses here and there sunk into the landscape
   forests at the edge of the fields poised to reclaim them
   no solid ground for miles, everything turns to mush
   hills like vast graves – the sun like a big dead eye—a dead Cyclops eye
   woods full of imaginary things—one big shadow now except where the sun shines across, splinters the shadow into thousands of twigs.
   I can't imagine a worse place for the imagination—the worst possible place for the imagination.

Moss's son Frank was there to meet me. [Moss runs the general store in Sloan.] Very tall. He works at the Woolworth's in Fairvale and just bought a car for himself. It had been raining all day, and after an hour or so on the road the downpour was so bad I wondered if we would have to stop. The road was badly rutted, I was thrown all over the back seat. Frank kept apologizing, saying that we'd get hopelessly stuck if we stopped at all. There were no streetlights, no light at all except for the headlights, and those were weak. With the rain I couldn't see anything. Frank's radio was broken—he tried to make conversation but we both had so little to say to each other. I started getting desperate, flying all over the back seat, I wanted to get out and ride on the running boards or on the hood—we had to keep the windows shut, it was raining so hard that even a tiny opening would drench us both. Frank kept wiping down the windshield, and asked me to do the same with the rear window.
   Finally I saw a few lights here and there, and I knew we'd arrived. We parked in front of the store and ran up to the porch. The rain was falling so hard it nearly knocked me down. We went in and had coffee—the store

looked a hundred years old. Moss is a big man, friendly. I was supposed to stay with him, but the basement room he had offered in his letter was flooded. We floundered around a bit, trying to figure out where I could stay—I was prepared to put up in his bathtub. Then Frank came in with Reverend Akerblom from the Lutheran church, which is only about a hundred yards from the store. He [Akerblom] offered to put me up in the church basement—on higher ground, still dry.

I'm here in the basement now.

Akerblom is not very old, still in his thirties. He uses an antique umbrella, the peaked kind. I didn't get a good look at the outside of the church, we were running, both hunched under his umbrella. Inside, very plain, very white. There's a door to one side of the podium that leads to his house, and a basement with a special guestroom. I'd be the first to use it since Miriam and Elie. Everything is clean and in order, like a hospital. Total quiet, except for the rain. One of the windows had been left open (there are two, close against the ceiling; they're the kind that hinges in the middle and swivels out, the glass is opaque, frosted) so it was freezing. Akerblom brought me a little heater. I put my suitcase on the bureau, under the open window, and looked out through the gap before I closed it. In the light from the chapel windows above me, I could see a few headstones close by. I was surprised there were so few. I've never looked up at headstones from below their level before—if I could see through the wall directly in front of me, I could see the coffins.

[Morning] I dreamt about something and now I don't remember, something very disturbing, all I can think of is a sort of blue color, like moonlight but bluer, like underwater light. Every time I think of that light I feel like I'm going to start shaking and that I'm about to remember.

[Presumably evening] Had breakfast with Akerblom, who lives alone. I asked him if the graves outside were the only ones—if I could find my sister's grave. He told me that, while there were graves around the church, there was no graveyard as such. When I asked him where people were buried, he said "all over", and that he didn't know where she was buried.

I spent the day at their old house. Moss had the key. He said he'd show me her grave tomorrow, that he had to take inventory today because he sent out his orders at the same time every other week.

Houses all over, with paths, but no roads. At least half are deserted, falling in. Their house was up very high, no one else had taken it. I started shaking when I got to the porch. I had to force myself to open the door, and then I nearly fell over backward, the house was completely empty, and dark. I started thinking of Miriam all through the house, walking in and out of the rooms, up and down the stairs. I wanted to read her diary there, but it was too dark, and I was crying. I was torturing myself by going there, but I thought that it might be worth it if I could get a sense of her again, some objective sense of her, not a memory, not something from me, but something she left behind. Is it worth it—am I just prolonging it?

Akerblom was out when I got back, so I sat on the porch at Moss's and tried to read. The only thing I could manage was more of her diary. Akerblom came back after sunset and made dinner for me back at the church. I asked him about my sister's funeral—it was held in the church, above my room. She had lain there in her coffin, just a few feet over where I lie to sleep. I miss her. Everything is boring, worthless, sad without her.

[Morning] Dreamt that the hills were graves for giants, I could somehow see through the dirt, their bodies were lying there flat, naked, in blue light from before—like giant shipwrecks. I dreamt that the water nymphs from Miriam's story were swimming in and out of them as if they were shadows—they hadn't rotted, but they were dry and stiff and blue—the water nymphs are their maggots, I understood this in the dream, but somehow in a totally different sort of way, not feeding on them at all, but learning their secrets. I saw them plainly, they looked like white slugs with feathery feelers.

I just remembered that I saw Miriam lying there with them, in the middle of the giants, I could see her lying in a little space in the earth, in her coffin, very far off among the hills. I could just see it like a rectangle of space in the ground and she was lying flat inside it, with her hands at her sides and the blue light just barely lighting her.

There was something else, some feeling that I can't name, as if they were all submerged in the same feeling, the water nymphs' secret was the feeling that they all had, and that I felt then.

[The "water nymphs" are from a Penobscot legend, presumably Miriam got it from her husband and wrote about it in her diary. Briefly—an ambitious Penobscot boy named "Devil Fish" or "Octopus" was out canoeing with his friends one day when they were approached by two creatures in a stone boat. They looked like the boys, but their eyes were unusually close together and they had extremely large noses, which they shyly covered with their hands. The creatures led the boys to a Mohawk camp, the boys surprised the resting Mohawk warriors and killed them all, returning to their village with the scalps. As a result, "Devil Fish" was able to start up a clan of his own, realizing his dearest wish. He and the other boys called the creatures in the stone boat "water nymphs". According to Elie Herman's completed manuscript, they are the spirits "who give you what you want". My uncle's notion that the water nymphs look like slugs is an idiosyncrasy of his dream.]

I had breakfast with Akerblom again, asked him if he would come with me to Miriam's grave with Moss today. He demurred, saying that he had to attend to a sick woman back in the woods and wouldn't be back until evening. He told me he had been drafted before he attended seminary and had served as a medic in the army, showed me his uniform.

Moss took me to Miriam's grave. There really are tombstones all over the place, here and there among the trees, as if people had been buried where they fell. Moss explained that, during bad winters, people were often buried wherever it was most convenient, to minimize exposure, often in the lee of houses that are now long gone. Most of the stones are broken or too badly eroded to be read. Moss took me down into a tiny glen between two large hills, where a large house had once stood. The old wrought-iron fencing was salvaged and used to mark off an elevated plot with about a dozen graves. Miriam had been laid next to Elie.

I'm the first to visit the grave. Mother is too fragile to come all the way out here. We had sent money for the stone. I stood over the grave and Moss moved off. I thought of her lying there, beneath the stone, her face turned up toward mine through the intervening earth. I saw her as I had in my dream, blue and white in her stiff dress, with her hands at her sides, creased with heavy shadows, her eyes completely shadowed and dark, her lips slightly parted over her dry teeth. I seemed to see the pits of her eyes, filled in with powdery shadows. I tried to think of her lying flat, but again and again I pictured her with her back slightly arched, her chin thrown slightly back, her head tilted slightly back—I started gasping again and I felt all the blood drain from my head, I fell forward on my knees, landing on the grass and I was pressing my hands into the grass. Moss and I walked back without saying anything.

We headed back to the store. I felt drained, like I was already forgetting everything that I missed about her. Even back at her grave I didn't feel as much as I thought I should—I wasn't as overwhelmed as I thought I'd be—but at the same time I feel as if a part of me demands not just that I try to keep this feeling alive to do justice to Miriam or to whatever it may be, but that something is still there, insisting that it's still there, as if life didn't end with life and there's still a beating heart there underground. Or not even that—it's enough that they're there—graveyards cast their spells without having to do anything. I could think these cold thoughts even after just visiting my sister's grave. This whole town is a graveyard.

Anyway, coming back to the store, I saw Reverend Akerblom off in the far distance, through a thin patch among the trees, walking with his umbrella, away from the church. Moss said he must be heading out to see Alice Pitcher, who I guess is his sick woman friend, but why was he heading out that way only now? Moss thought he had other people to see as well.

Akerblom came back a little after sunset and we had dinner together. He seemed upset.

I read the diary over and over again. I miss her. But all this is so overwhelming, more exhausting every day.

[Morning] Last night—I was lying in bed looking at the light around the door, at the strip of light under the door, and there was a gap, a shadow right in the middle, as if someone was standing directly in front of the door, not moving. I lay there and looked at it for hours. Then I fell asleep, or looked away, and when I looked again, Miriam was standing there, leaning her back against the door, with her hands at her sides—she didn't move or speak, she just stood there watching me, her face was glowing very faintly a blue color and her eyes were pits, and she had no expression on her face, she didn't look like herself, she didn't look like anybody—I was strangling, the blankets were hot and damp and weighing down on me and I couldn't move. Then she came to life, came across to the bed and leaned over me, looking much more like herself now, I couldn't see her eyes but I could see them glistening—in the moonlight from the window, which might have been open. She was leaning right over me and maybe half kneeling where she stood, and she reached down and moved the blanket down a little, and she slid her hand just inside the top of my shirt, which was unbuttoned there, and she parted it with her hand and laid her palm lightly on my bare chest. Her hand was cool, but it grew warm as it lay on my chest. I felt her weight pressing down on the mattress next to me, and I reached up and pulled her down to me, I could feel her body through the stiff material of her dress, compact inside her dress—she leaned down to me and kissed me, flowed over me like cool water, her lips were cool and soft and very moist and her face glowed and I warmed it with my breath as I kissed her—she undressed me almost without moving, but I remember how her hands grew warm as she took my clothes off—then I lunged up and swung her down under me, and suddenly she was naked, she drew my face down to her throat—she was perfumed with water—she held me and gave me everything I'd always wanted, it went on for hours and hours, her head was tilted back, her eyes and mouth made three black glistening crescents against her white face, her lips were just parted over her teeth, surging frenziedly against me down below and I was just throwing myself ravenously on her like I was going to eat her up, until she quenched me, I remember thinking it was like plunging hot iron into cold water, and I looked down at her beneath me and thought how I'd fallen on her grave with my hands outstretched, and thought triumphantly to myself—there's no earth between us now! and laughed out loud, and her entire body shook with laughter in my arms. I watched her smile—I remember watching it spread slowly across her face, the corners of her mouth drawing slowly back, and the laughter came flashing out between her teeth that gleamed like pearls in her dark mouth. Her straight dark hair spread in a sheet across the pillow, very dark, the pillow very light, darker and lighter, I plunged my face into her hair that smelled like fresh ice and her arms cinched tighter around me pulling me completely inside and down into her. When I woke up I was alone, completely alone.

My God I slept for eighteen hours.

I have nothing to say I can't say anything about it, I can't think about anything, I just don't have it in me anymore, I'm just putting it away, out of sight for now.

[That Afternoon] When I got up it was already afternoon, and there was a note from Akerblom saying he'd be out—I started walking toward Miriam's grave and then I saw him [Akerblom] on the path, more or less where I saw him yesterday, far ahead of me and moving off into the hills. I followed him but I couldn't catch up, he was moving too quickly, and then I lost him around a corner, I simply rounded the bend and he wasn't there. It took me a few moments, but I found the spot where he'd left the path, taking off directly through the trees, heading down into the glens.

I followed and stopped up short behind a tree when I saw him, he was below me, with his umbrella up. He was standing on a sort of rocky bank by the ruins of what looked like an old farmhouse set leaning right up against the hillside. The house itself was gone, but the cellar was still intact, flooded. A sort of mudslide had roofed it over, so that it appeared to jut right out from the base of the hill, pressing up against a four foot bank, and the bottom of the glen where it stood was flooded with still black water. Akerblom was up on the bank with his umbrella, and I stopped when I heard him, because he was speaking to someone. I could barely see the door to the cellar over the bank—only the top of the door and about a quarter of one side. Inside it was pitch black, but then I realized there was someone standing just inside the door—whoever it was was either very tall or standing on something, if he wasn't he was at least knee-deep in water, I could only see his head and shoulders, and that only through the doorway, he looked a little like Akerblom, but he kept the lower half of his face covered with his hands all the time!

He's been talking with them every day, at least since I got here and perhaps from before! I watched him, he just stood there stiff as a board and talked with them—I could hear his voice but not the other's. I couldn't see its eyes, at least not both at once, it swayed in and out of the door. I noticed there were ripples in the water around the bank, the water that had flooded the cellar, and it occurred to me that those ripples were coming from the cellar, that the water must have backed up from under the ground in the cellar and poured out, not the other way around, and I could see that I was right from the lay of the land, the cellar was a little elevated. It was obvious, too, why the farmhouse had been demolished by the slide, and why the cellar had been claimed by the hill—how far back into the hill does it go? Where does the water come from if not deep back under the hills, among the graves—there were graves even this far out, I'm sitting next to a headstone right now, not leaning against it, but I'm sitting near one. When I realized what he was doing, who he was talking to, I sneaked away up the hill to hide in the trees here and write this—now more than ever it's important for me to write down everything.

I came up here and sat down, and I saw the headstone for the first time only a few minutes ago. The dead are everywhere, they're "all over" like Akerblom said, everywhere you go there's someone else—not anybody in particular, just Someone there under the ground! I sat here and stared at that stone without moving, and thought of all of them. Then I seemed to see Miriam coming up the hill toward me, slowly. I imagined she came up to where I was and sat down next to me, and laid her hand on mine, and smiled at me. Just like this morning I'm completely alone, there's nothing for me now but these endless graves and Miriam's company, and now as I sit and think about it, alone as I am, I'm surrounded by a host of people underground. My dream last night, and the others, all came from them, as a way of promising her to me, and Akerblom knows about it and has been going out there every day to stop me, because he knows I won't go down to see them while he's there. But now that I know that they're real nothing is going to stop me from coming back again and again—he can't be here every waking moment.

[Later] They're still talking. I just remembered I have to go back into town and talk to Frank, he thinks he's taking me home tomorrow morning. I should stay but now I think of going down there, I think of Miriam, but— what would it look like, how would I talk to it? A moment ago I was so angry at Akerblom I was ready to do anything to defy him, but now I feel I'm starting to shake—I have to come back later, when the sun is higher in the sky.

[Later] Akerblom left my dinner for me and went out again without saying more than half a dozen words to me. I watched him leave—he went down to Moss's. He's angry—I'm sure he suspects. Am I supposed to stay here without knowing what he's thinking of me? Moss said his basement was flooded—does that mean they're down there too? What if the church basement floods? My head is filling up with idiotic contemptible ideas—I should go out and see them right now, I can't go, I took one step in that direction and I froze, I can feel them pulling at me, if I started on that way I'd be giving in, I wouldn't be able to stop myself, I'd walk right down into that cellar, they wouldn't have to listen to me, they could do whatever they wanted to with me. You have to be strong and cunning, and control yourself, come back when the sun is high in the sky and we can't help but listen. Think of Miriam and keep yourself under control. Go to bed early, get up early, and beat Akerblom to it.

[Morning] Briefly—

I saw her standing in the cellar doorway, with her hands on the sill, shouting my name, then I saw past her to where the water comes up, and I saw them—like slugs with feathery antennae, almost six feet or so, swimming like seals in the water, just under the surface, coming and going from further inside the hill, all white but gleaming with different colors as if they were filmed with oil or sheathed in prismatic glass, and their bodies were blazing and flickering—they aren't made of flesh, they're made of static, they move through the water and the soil. The ones in the cellar took me aside and waved their hands, showed me the whole landscape for miles around with the earth stripped away, and I saw miles and miles of tiny human bodies hanging suspended where the soil had been, lying flat all over, at crazy angles, and I saw other gigantic bodies sprawled where the hills had been, where the water nymphs spawned, moving through them like fish in and out of a shipwreck, where they had been deliberately buried, the first people, and then the second, the Indians coming in, walking in the air above the graves, where the surface had been, in among the hovering trees, I realized this is how they see the world, the water and the earth, and us, putting bodies in the soil with care. The giant others loomed over the other graves, I saw Miriam lying there between them, and one of their faces was turned toward her, looming over the size of a house, soft half-closed eyes almost falling out from under their lids, a gouged, ruined mouth and vast yellow teeth gaping—the cellar I saw opened directly onto a cavernous chest, piles of soft blue-white entrails glistening white and multicolored as if they were sheathed in prismatic glass, and then again I saw Miriam standing in the doorway to the cellar shouting my name, calling me out to her again.

[Later] Akerblom locked me in—that son of a bitch locked me in my room! He was awake before me, I overslept through my alarm if it ever went off, but when I came up to get breakfast he was there, told me he was staying in today to work on his sermon for Sunday and went back into his office—the second I come back down here to get my coat the door slams behind me and the key turns in the lock! I've been trying to break it down but nothing—I'm going to try to get the window open, I'll break it if I have to, and yell for help—I'm writing this down so that everyone will know what happened if anything happens to me—

Yelled—nothing—Now I'm coming over nauseous, sweating, my skin's on fire, I was stupid enough to eat the food he left out for me! I'm going to hide this, let whoever finds it know that Akerblom poisoned me, gag myself, I swear if I live through this I'll kill him, and I'll throw him down in the cellar for them to have so they'll have to listen to me.

[The diary ends here.]

As far as I could tell, my uncle was evacuated from Sloan that day by ambulance, made a full recovery, and never went back or mentioned the affair to anyone. Reverend Akerblom is still alive, although he doesn't answer my letters—I know this from Frank Moss with whom I've had a couple of conversations over the new and as yet only Sloan phone line, connected at the General Store. Here's my paraphrase of his account of that day:

Reverend Akerblom came running down to the store that morning in a hurry. He said that William Slaite had fallen unexpectedly ill and that he needed the doctor immediately. Unfortunately, Dr. Masson, the town doctor, was away tending to Alice Pitcher that day and was basically out of reach for the time being. Akerblom believed that my uncle had an unusually abrupt and violent appendicitis, and feared that he was due to rupture and hemorrhage within a few hours—in light of the emergency, Akerblom volunteered to remove my uncle's appendix himself—he had served as a medic in the army, and had been trained to perform a few very simple operations. Luckily, the doctor was due to get some fresh medical supplies that day, the parcel was simply sitting there at the post office counter in the store. Akerblom enlisted Frank Moss' help in getting the box up to the church and in the operation. In the meantime, Moss would drive into Fairvale to get help from the hospital there (which would take the better part of the day).

Frank said that my uncle was bathed in sweat, his face was burning up when he touched it, and that he was delirious, muttering, lying on his bed in the basement guestroom. They sterilized the room as best they could—Akerblom instructed Frank quickly on how to keep my uncle chloroformed during the operation, and began the operation quickly. Frank admitted he'd been too squeamish to watch, keeping his back turned, concentrating on my uncle and the chloroform. He felt that Akerblom blamed himself for my uncle's condition, he cursed and muttered incomprehensibly to himself under his breath during the entire operation.

Frank lost track of time. He came to when Akerblom clapped him on the back and congratulated him. There was a small stitched incision in my uncle's side, but otherwise all seemed well—his fever started dropping almost immediately, but he did not regain consciousness.

That night, the ambulance finally arrived. Dr. Masson had still not returned. Moss and Frank helped pack up my uncle's things and load up the ambulance. At one point, as Frank was looking around to make sure they'd left nothing behind, he noticed my uncle's diary lying hidden under the mattress in the guest-room. Apparently, when Akerblom saw it he nearly snatched it out of Frank's hands in front of Moss and both the ambulance attendants. According to Frank, Akerblom seemed upset to see it, and asked if he could look at it a moment. Rather than look at it, he actually took it aside and bound it with twine, sealed it with wax and the impression of his ring, as I had found it, before returning it to Frank to put among my uncle's things. According to Frank, Akerblom explained only by saying "I'm doing him a favor."

My uncle was examined at the hospital in Fairvale and found to be in good condition, apparently Reverend Akerblom's operation had been a complete success. However, he did not regain consciousness, apparently due to profound exhaustion. At my mother's request, he was moved by helicopter to a Portland hospital, where he awoke the next morning. To all appearances, his mind was an almost total blank regarding Miriam, Sloan, or Reverend Akerblom, his benefactor. The operation itself left only the faintest possible scar.

What He Chanced to Mould in Play

It was a city named New York, in a part of the city named Coney Island. I ventured there in a state of nervous exasperation. Not knowing where to go, I had been standing there on the street fuming, impatient to get away anywhere, when something caught my attention. Something appeared in the sky; it was a sort of break in the clouds, it was dusk … and in the break in the clouds I could see some bit of vapor lit by the red rays of the sun, looking like a single coil of red intestine up there. Then the idea, that I should go to Coney Island, came into my head.

The train station was awash in ammonia and water. On the street, I passed a row of garages that various persons were using as ad hoc shops. All sorts of rubbish slopped out onto the sidewalk and on card tables. I saw the rides and the midway I suppose it's called and made my way to the boardwalk. The rides were deserted, but a number of young people, boys mostly, idled there between the rides. A rollercoaster creaked and groaned as the heavy car went by.

I climbed onto the boardwalk. The little hot dog places were shuttered, their walls plastered with pornographic paintings of clams, hot dogs, hamburgers, pizza slices, the bill of faire. The nearly deserted shooting gallery was still open. Every now and then a fugitive crack or whine could be heard above the laughter of the seagulls. The wind was brisk, the sea very calm on the rocks. I ventured out onto the cross-shaped pier. People were fishing in the unwholesome water; I saw many small caches of crabs with feebly waving legs.

When I turned to face inland, I could see a thunderstorm sweeping over the city. The rain fell in a tin-colored fringe, and I heard thunder. Roughly opposite the pier was a derelict roller coaster; its paint had long chipped away, leaving it black and brown; it had been fenced off, and vines were growing all over it. In every respect, it reminded me of a dinosaur skeleton, slouching there, half-erect, half slumped to the ground like rotting ribs. As I walked down the pier toward it, I saw a bolt of violet lightning bisect its inverted arch. The lightning had struck far off, its sound wafted surprisingly gently over me a moment later, but for a moment it stood there, making a W out of the roller coaster's giant U. As I came nearer, it happened again.

There was a smear of sand across the wooden boards of the pier, and little dark divots and spots were opening in it. The rain was starting to fall here on the beach. People cantored by me with their sweaters and jackets held over their heads; I could see many already sheltering beneath the awnings of the hot dog stands. As it wasn't raining in earnest yet, I stood at the railing of the boardwalk and studied the old roller coaster. It was surrounded by an area of recently cleared brush, most of which was heaped up immediately before me: a mass of plowed-up greenery and dirt mixed with blankets and towels, shoes, cans, newspaper … There was a house incorporated into the roller coaster; it stood beneath and apparently helped to support it.

Facing me, the house was two stories tall and shaped much like a barn. A patriotic flag hung from one side, where I presumed the front door to be. Most of the paint had been stripped from the battleship colored wood, the windows were fogged with dust, but one of them, on the upper right, exhibited a new flowered curtain. I wandered over to a small flight of steps and walked along the street bordering the lot. A few dozen feet from the boardwalk, the fencing was bowed inward where a great deal of weight had pressed the chain-link to the ground. The house would be haunted by more of the surly young men I had seen earlier. Naturally, I had a closer look.

The house was old and sodden, like a soggy cardboard box. It smelled strongly of mildew and the earwax odor that old houses generally have. The rain was beginning to fall more seriously now. I was greeted by a brown man, who invited me inside through a gash in the wall. He was rather nattily dressed, with a greenish woolen jacket and a claret-colored bow tie, and his squeaking leather shoes glinted. The room into which he beckoned me was oblong, spacious. In addition to the mercurial light from outside, the room was illuminated by a number of paper-shaded electric candles in wall sconces. Faded threadbare carpets, a few armchairs trailing entrails of wadding and springs, a low table and some smaller, taller tables, a cavernous fireplace, and even some paintings on the wall.

The brown man was shorter than I, with a receding hairline, his remaining hair was black, stiff, closely cut. There were deep, thin creases in his face. He looked like a jovial Middle Eastern academic. The rain had stopped when I entered the house, but now the presence of this man made leaving awkward, and had besides aroused my curiosity. Although he seemed to belong to the place, I asked him if he had been caught in the rain.

"I didn't come here for shelter, if that's what you mean.—You are—?" He turned to me, with his hands clasped behind his back, wanting to pick up my name as it were without losing momentum; I knew he would repeat it when I said it, and then continue his thought.

"My name is Thot."

"Mr. Thot, that's good! I am studying here, that is I am studying *here*, this place." He made a gesture a bit like dropping his hands onto typewriter or piano keys to indicate here, and then put his hands behind his back again. "My name is Arlath. This is a very interesting place. I think that this was once a worshipping-place; a secret worshipping-place. Perhaps it still is. Take a look at this."

He gestured me over to a painting he had evidently removed from the wall

115

and set up across the arms of a wooden chair.

"What do you think?"

The painting had a heavy, ponderously carved golden frame with a brass plate at the bottom that read only "A. D. S."

I asked him about "A. D. S.", but he only urged me first to give the painting my careful scrutiny.

It was almost completely black, although whether this was as it had been painted, or was simply the accumulated grime of many years, I couldn't tell. The oil paint was thick, applied to the canvas with a palette knife as well as a brush. The strokes were sweeping, sinuous, torturous, while the palette strokes were staccato, ridgy whorls, all mysterious colors; I noted especially a transparent oceanic blue-green that held deeper notes of purple. What was represented, if anything, was a seething obscurity. The oils gleamed, adding weirdly harmonious lights to the dark, plastic *thing* they made.

"I think that this is a portrait of God," Mr. Arlath said to me. "And that people once met, may still meet, regularly in this house, to worship what you see there. It is a terribly old cult. Come sit here with me."

We sat facing each other in two of the slouching armchairs. Their gutted condition made it necessary for us to sit perched on the edges of the seats. The painting stood on its own chair, adjacent to us both.

"You may be familiar with the idea that life, all of what exists, was caused to come into being by some personal act of creation on the part of a divine being. This is a nearly ubiquitous belief. In most cases, this supposed act of creation is deliberate, and the resulting universe takes shape according to a pre-established plan. However, there are some instances of this belief in which it is held, on the contrary, that the act of creation was inadvertent. Some believe that the act of creation was not simply inadvertent, but took place unnoticed by the creator. Now we approach another, related belief, that life is a dream. Most who believe this, believe the dream is their own dream. But some believe that life, and the totality of existence, is the unwitting dream of a divine being. Like you and I, this being dreams without knowing he dreams, without even paying much attention to these dreams.

"Now consider the eschatology that this implies. We know that dreams don't last, are fleeting, that is in the nature of dreams. So, if everything that exists is a dream, then we can expect the dreamer to wake up, and everything in existence to disappear. Some expect that this waking up will take place right away, and that we who are elements in the great dream will vanish immediately, without ever being aware of our nature. But others picture a more gradual awakening, when, for those of us who are conscious elements in the great dream, things will begin to dwindle, lose their substance, and we will dwindle with them. The dream always takes its substance, so to speak, from the dreamer. As the dream unravels, it returns its borrowed substance to the dreamer; in particular, those fragments of the dreaming consciousness will return to their source, disappearing one by one, until the dreamer awakens entirely, and is alone.

"This spot is consecrated to the observation of that dream, the worship of the dreamer and the dreamer's messenger, who is the first facet of his consciousness, and the facilitator or fabricator of the dream. This messenger figure is common in religions all around the world; knowing the dream, having built the dream, and in a certain sense being the dream, he is able to impart to those who only approximately understand the true nature of reality what would seem to be the secrets of the universe, what are the secrets of the dream. And just as he is the one who creates and sustains the dream, so it is his responsibility to undo the dream when it is time for the dreamer to awaken, as it is in the nature of dreams to end.

"Now listen carefully."

He takes a business card from his jacket pocket and shows it to me, his eyes locked on mine. He then takes a pen from the breast pocket of his shirt and writes on the card, holding it up for me to see. Before his name he has written N Y, and after his name he has written O T E P. He shows me this, and stares into my eyes. Then he writes again on the card, and holds it up a second time. He has written my name. He writes again on the card and holds it up a third time. He has written N Y A R L A before my name, and E P after my name.

"The messenger," he says, trying to call it out of my memory.

"The message," he says. He writes again on the card, my name, then writes again and holds up the card. Before my name, A Z A, after my name, the letter H.

I am alone.

The Ice Age of Dreams.

While I didn't set out to write a pastiche of T. E. D. Klein's work, I did want to get some of his flavoring into this one, and some Machen as well. After Tuey made his debut in "Firebrands of Torment", I thought he might make a decent narrator.

Ice Age of Dreams

for Thomas Ligotti

"I am in the awkward position of a man who has made it his business to speak and write about a kind of experience, the experience of occult matters, about which no true witness ever speaks or writes. The few who genuinely do go beyond the circle of human firelight, and who return, are either unwilling or unable to give voice to their discoveries. Having come back, they are not, as a rule, so interested in trivia, or so avid in pursuit of a futile communication with closed minds, as to account for their experiences. For this reason, most occult libraries are fragmentary; they are compelled from so many bits and pieces produced in a state of ephemeral optimism as to the possibility of transmissibility; and these disassociated fragments can not generally be made to cohere: their truth lies in the gaps between them.

"'The oldest and strongest emotion of mankind is fear, and the oldest and strongest kind of fear is fear of the unknown.' Those words stare up, not at me, but into the air from off the page lying open beside me at my desk. The man who wrote them once sounded a word of warning about the possibility of other minds than ours, that could very well be the final truth behind the mystery of Divinity. There is no doubt that individual persons have known them or known of them, but, in this case, that is the only thing that is not in doubt."

—Arthur Hennepin Tuey,
from the *Tuey Occult Quarterly*, #237

Doctor Brunno Hennel has died. A universally respected colleague, a visionary, upon his death the institutions that did everything in their power to destroy him in life called him "an indispensable man in his field." I knew him, though only through correspondence. His life was his work, and, for the sake of an appetite for knowledge that was innocent and disinterested, though no less powerful for that innocence, he placed his life in danger, and he died. Now, circumstances will begin to bury and contradict, all the blinding mechanisms of this world will hastily obscure, that which I will set down here as it is fresh in my mind. I have witnessed the truth of it.

120

Above this statement, I have attached the words I wrote to first introduce Bruno Hennel to my readers. Since then, I have put aside that bellicose language. I found myself in the even more "awkward position" of being an eye-witness. The vague and suggestive events that followed Hennel's death are being patiently wiped away, the few pieces of evidence disappearing. I have found the words of warning issuing from my own mouth.

I was first exposed to Dr. Hennel's work at a small academic conference, and it was my honor to be the first to publish his stunningly original dream monograph. The dream was his object; as he said, dreams were a "primary substance."

"Every intimation of what borders what is known and intelligible comes in dreams, and there is no good reason to assume that dreams are not what they so clearly appear to be: manifestations of another life.

"My goal in this paper is to lay the foundation for a natural history of dreams. I will argue, on ground prepared by my own experiments with self-hypnosis and hypnosis of trance subjects, and by my research into relevant historical material, including passages from *The History of Mur* and the *Hidden Rose*, that dreams are visitation, and are at least capable of independent existence."

With the meager resources he was able to command from the university, where I should add his reputation in anthropological circles was soon completely ruined, he had pursued his research with tireless dedication on his own time. Hennel invented the new theory of transpersonal dreaming, and appeared to prove that, under some circumstances, dreams exhibited both recognizable, non-psychological behavior, and could even persist in registering on his equipment after the disconnection and departure of the test dreamer. The results appeared first in my Quarterly.

When the university betrayed him, terminating his contract with the most insulting allegations, he, with his usual good will, simply proceeded to accumulate new resources. This effort consumed much of his time, and I had not heard from Hennel in years when I received his unexpected telephone call. I was more surprised by his tone. He sounded as if he were speaking at some distance from the receiver, although the sound was clear.

He said he was in a phone booth by the interstate, near a town in the north whose name I withhold—it would mean nothing to any of you now, even if it was once your hometown. I heard no traffic. Only crickets, and the sounds of nocturnal insects. Hennel was speaking very quietly, calmly. I could sense the effort to be calm. He spoke almost continuously; I interjected very little.

"I've been pursuing more traditional lines of research ... This area is mentioned in the body of some native folklore, very old stories ..."

I was unable to catch many of the references he made. I remember asking him some clarifying questions—though there was something precarious in his voice that made me hesitant to speak.

"Well … I've been exploring the idea of *fossilized* dreams, some traces … These would be ancient dreams, that were caused to solidify over time … completely independent, material dreams …"

There was a longer pause.

"… I'm calling to report … I've succeeded …"

I heard a car pass.

Hennel explained. He had been digging in a spot not too far from town, screened by rock outcrops and heavy timber. I never learned the precise location. Shortly before sunset, he had found them.

"… They were buried in what appeared to be rows … like the terracotta soldiers in China … a series of small mounds apparently in rows … I had to work quickly—the sun was going down … I uncovered the first of the mounds … I did some digging and then worked with the brush … I found myself brushing a smooth … and slightly pale … surface … marked with … a few fine grooves … I cleared more earth away …"

The line was silent for a few seconds.

"… What came out … it was like an apparition … I could see the features … I had been brushing at the … forehead … and then I saw the rest of the face …"

Though his tone was measured and his voice was steady, Hennel sounded fragile. I expected his voice to shatter in panic at any moment. At first he believed he had uncovered a buried cadaver, but, Hennel said,

"It was something like a statue … man-sized … partially formless … it was a … a *solid dream* … the face was … shining from out of a low mound … one of many mounds …"

I sat in my apartment, in the solitary light of my desk-lamp, and from out of the receiver came the sound of another far-away night, passing cars, crickets, and Hennel's faint voice speaking calmly—illusory calm.

"… I found … I couldn't look at … the face … not once it was exposed … but even without looking at it … I could feel its … gaze, or its presence … it had … a palpable gaze … like heat …"

I asked him something, I had the feeling he was slipping into a sort of reverie—and that he had called me deliberately with the intention of *preventing* that reverie. He seemed to become more alert.

"… The sun was setting … I had to leave so I photographed it with … an instant camera … I have the photo now.

"—Tuey … do you believe me? … Do you think I've lost my mind somehow?"

We spoke for some time; he seemed to relax, and some of his enthusiasm seemed to return. He repeated referred to the photograph, whose presence troubled him, and said that he was both strongly drawn to look at it, and profoundly repelled by it. He said that he might burn it, and the idea afforded him some relief.

After our conversation, I sat a long time at my desk. The distractions of the city outside were very helpful.

Hennel had promised to telephone me the next day. Eight days passed before I heard from him again. My telephone rang in the late afternoon and the voice that came from the receiver was so slurred and stammering that I had trouble recognizing it. I repeatedly asked Hennel to tell me about his condition. Eventually he said that he was still in that northern town. He was trying to tell me something about his discoveries, but he seemed to be groping for words, as in a dream, and I found myself losing track of his sentences in the many long silences.

"I went back there ..." Hennel said. "... nothing but ... an enormous sinkhole ... the figures ... none of the figures were there ... absolutely all ... were not there ..."

I asked about the photograph.

"Yes ... ? Yes ... I still have it ... I'm looking at it now ..."

He returned repeatedly, for reasons that weren't clear to me then, to the calendar.

"Tuey ... you know the seasons ... the Greek 'kairos', the proper time? ... the moon now is ... just leaving ... I'm sorry ... just leaving the new phase ..."

I told Hennel that he sounded unwell and should leave that town immediately, possibly visit a doctor. He seemed to take this advice to heart, but in the end, Hennel said that he felt overwhelmed and incapable, and begged me to come and get him.

He had no family, and I was one of his small circle of acquaintances—I did not want to leave Hennel there. Difficult as traveling is for me, refusing to help Hennel was out of the question.

Train service to that place had been long discontinued. I traveled by rail as far as I could and rented a car at the final station. I already knew I was voyaging toward a dying destination. Shipping trade had made it a boom town, now the trade had passed by and the citizens were slowly moving on to new places themselves. The surrounding countryside had remained empty, waiting for suburbs that, unneeded after all, were never built. I came upon the town through low hills to the south, bristling with ancient trees. I passed a turn-off with a rest stop and several phone booths, and I knew that this was the point of origin for Hennel's first call. Houses came up around me, but I had no sense of place at all. Finally, here and there I saw desultory threads of people going about their daily business, mothers with perambulators, children coming home from school, persons milling in and out of a supermarket and a gas station. To see these things, this stupid consumerism, this everyday drabness, that I normally so abhor, and to be as relieved to see them as I was then, I never expected.

I contacted Hennel on the telephone in the filling station, and arranged to meet him in front of the rooming house where he was staying. The drive took me through deserted, watchful neighborhoods in the center of town; striking, odd little buildings unlike anything in the outskirts, neglected – but they had a way of obtruding on the eye, demanding my attention so that I found it difficult to follow the narrow lanes. I found myself anxiously watching the gauges on the dashboard, irrationally afraid of breaking down or getting stuck some way in a cul-de-sac. As I turned, I remembered later on, I caught a brief glimpse of a small group of people in the street behind my car, all dressed in pale grey. They were dressed something like Mennonites, and seemed to belong to the inner city I had left.

Hennel came down to meet me. I waited for some time in front of the house, actually an old hotel on a garden circle; the sun had already set by the time he appeared. Hennel looked fatigued in the weak light of the streetlamps, but he greeted me warmly. On his suggestion we walked together up the street, two lumbering, unwell old men.

This was the Hennel of the first phone call again, calm and more prone to lecture than to converse back and forth. We stood closely together and he spoke continuously in a low tone. The streetlights were pale and not numerous, the moon was dark, the sidewalk patched with heavy blots of shadow from the trees. I glanced at him from time to time, but for the most part we walked facing forward. In the dark, I could see the glistening of his eyes and the motion of his features as he spoke.

"I want to apologize to you … I genuinely didn't know what to do. Those alarming phone calls must have—well, I don't imagine it was very pleasant for you …"

I said something, asked about his health, and he waved my questions aside with his hands. Hennel paused for some time before speaking again.

"Strange thing, I am unable to decide whether or not I want to leave … I haven't stopped working, even though I knew you were coming … I've done some more experiments, under the obvious limitations here … and I feel a breakthrough is very close. —But, at the same time … this place makes me tired …" he rubbed his eyes, "… and nervous," he added, sighing.

Hennel seemed inclined to leave with me, wanting me to allay his doubts about abandoning his project. I told him, as frankly as I could, that I thought he was exhibiting signs of an immanent breakdown, and should leave, and suspend his studies, for the time being.

"Breakdown or breakthrough are my choices, and maybe that's not a choice," he said.

His more professorial tone intervened. "I hope you don't mind my using you as a test audience, Tuey, but I'm afraid I'm thinking out loud these days. You'll have to bear with me—the thoughts are still disorganized."

Whenever Hennel discussed complicated ideas, ideas that were still being articulated, he spoke slowly, with great deliberation and emphasis.

"... You already understand that ... dreams cycle in time, fluctuate in time, with lunar phases and times of year, and so on ... dream visitations coincide with ... and depend upon ... a window of opportunity determined by the prevailing temporal complexion ... the time when these dreams come through is strictly determined ... and there are also ... cycles of greater duration and ... correspondingly greater magnitude of effect ... that would be something like ... ice ages in geological terms ... periods of overall—" Hennel was straining to speak, "—of total, sweeping changes ... in dreams ..."

Then Hennel seized my arm in the dark.

"... My research has ... indicated ... that the ... figures I have uncovered ... are fossilized remains of such a ... past age ... and that ... given the vast amount of time involved ... I must conclude that they are ... of *inhuman* origin."

I asked him what he meant.

Hennel said, "I mean ... I am certain those dreams were not *human dreams* ... Tuey—for *other minds*," he said.

We walked together. I glanced up through the branches.

Hennel spoke. "I can not elaborate yet ... given time, I think I can produce more proof."

I asked him about the photograph, with a strange feeling.

Hennel hesitated. "I will show you," he said, "but not now—I left it in my room anyway."

By this time, we had emerged onto one of the few remaining service streets. In the lights of the storefronts I could see that Hennel was appallingly pale, his features tensed. He only smiled weakly when I expressed concern, and bade me go on with him. I was going to protest, when he seized my arm a second time and began to speak about the sectarians. When I began to follow what he was saying, I realized he was talking about the people who lived in the inner city, the ones who wore pale grey.

"Frankly, I am *obsessed* with those people," he said. Abruptly, he turned and said, "Will you excuse me—I'm feeling a little unwell ... I know this place here ..."

Hennel had stopped in front of a second-hand book store, now he stepped gingerly inside.

The man behind the counter knew Hennel and they exchanged greetings. I followed Hennel into the stacks toward the back of the store. There was a bathroom in a sort of closet behind the rearmost shelves; "Romances," said an index card on a tack. Hennel paused just a moment, with his back to me and his hand on the door jam, before going in.

I ambled, not going far, looking at the stacks. Unstained wood, paperbacks, stale cigarette smoke, a low ceiling blazing with fluorescents strung on corrugated metal connectors, some small speakers through which the radio behind the register was changing stations. There was a brief flare of static as the door opened in the back of the shop, some distance, by then, from where I was standing. I watched Hennel step slowly into the aisle, his face terribly white, and damp with perspiration. I walked toward Hennel. He took a few steps, looking at the floor, faintly panting and swallowing. Hennel lay down on the floor, on his side. When I reached him, and turned him on his back, he was dead.

I rode with Hennel in the ambulance. He had already been pronounced dead in the bookstore, his body was covered. My friend had turned into an object. I sat beside him, across from the attendant, who had given up trying to make conversation.

In the store, I had turned from Hennel's body, calling for help and rushing to the counter. I remembered the shocked face of the man behind the register; then I remembered what I saw over his shoulder, through the shop window, as he dialed the telephone. On the empty sidewalk across the street, I saw someone passing by—he had almost slipped my memory, but, in the ambulance, I remembered. He was a sectarian, dressed in pale grey, and he passed under the streetlight directly opposite the second-hand bookstore. He walked by at a steady pace, with his face tilted downwards and his eyes fixed on the sidewalk, and as he passed he lifted his hand and tipped his hat. He tipped his hat on an empty sidewalk.

I suppose I gasped. The attendant was looking at me with alarm, as if I were going to collapse next.

Hennel had no family; I was the only one in a position to make arrangements. I spent the rest of the evening numbly filling out forms. The hospital was nearly empty, and quiet. Around ten o'clock the pathologist proclaimed that Hennel had died of a stroke. It was too late for me to find a room of my own in town, and I had no inclination to return to Hennel's rooming house; one of the candy stripers suggested I take advantage of one of the hospital's many empty rooms. I took her advice, selecting a room on the second floor, facing the hills. When I removed my coat, I found the photograph in my outside pocket.

Hennel and I had been walking all but arm-and-arm earlier that evening. There is no telling how much he had suspected—I thought again of the sectarian tipping his hat.

Now I was looking at Hennel's photograph. I saw only a patch of brilliant pallor framed by a disturbed earth, at first. As I examined it more closely, I saw the features. Together they were a blank, bare face, with the neutral expression of a portrait bust. Even in the wash of light the details were extraordinary and clear, the substance unblemished after what I gathered was a long burial. I looked attentively at Hennel's photograph, and it was only then, with prolonged examination, that I saw the *cast* of those features—not at all neutral, not at all blank, but subtly arrogant, ironic, the gaze of the irisless eyes palpably slid around me, as if they disdained to meet mine, and so unlike stone, so much like a face arrested only by the stillness of the photograph itself, that I realized what Hennel had meant when he said the figure was only *like* a statue. It was neither a statue nor a mummy, but between. Hennel had said he could feel the presence of that face, like heat, even when his back was turned. I imagined it in the dark of the deserted forest, its contemptuous light falling on the trees. And I thought, not even Hennel had the slightest idea where that face had gone. And there were many more low mounds, a whole regiment down there, now disappeared.

I realized I had been drawing Hennel's photograph steadily closer to my face. I needed to stop a moment and catch my breath, tear my eyes from that unwholesome face. I clapped it into the binding of my notebook. Hennel had said he was troubled by the very presence of the photograph itself. I was not readily able to sleep knowing it was in the room with me, and there was no question of extinguishing the lights.

In the end, I could not keep Hennel's photograph. I know I should have kept it but I couldn't bear to have it. It gnaws as me in my memory, and its presence was intolerable. I did not destroy it, however—it is Hennel's sole proof, the sole proof of this story now, provided it still exists. For my own peace of mind, I have secreted it, such that even I do not know exactly where it is. I do know that, should the need arise, I could lay my hands on it again, through channels. That is, provided it, unlike the other evidence of these events, has not also gone away.

I spent a bad night at that hospital. In the morning, fatigued and disturbed as I was, I decided to remain in that town some time longer. I completed the arrangements for Hennel. He had already mentioned his preference for cremation to me.

I found myself on the sidewalk, in front of the hospital, at a loss. A cab brought me back to my car, and to Hennel's rooming house; we went the long way round, at my request. His bill was small, and I settled it. I found his room ajar, and for an outraged moment I wondered if it had been searched—if it had, I never knew. I found no notes, only the few sad remains, mostly rubbish. The windows were closed, the curtains drawn, the air in the room was stale. The bed disheveled, where he had lain only a short while ago.

Later, while driving in circles, I found the local historical society, housed in a peeling three-story Victorian with a great sweep of brown lawn. The place was deserted except for an earnest, scholarly young man in a white suit, who greeted me with great surprise on the stairs. We sat and drank coffee in the barren kitchen of the house.

I asked him directly about the sectarians, without pursuing the lie I had concocted in the car about writing some sort of newspaper story. The young man gave me a brief history of the town, the life and death of the inner city.

"Business died, rents dropped, and even the older buildings, some of which date from the first settlement, became just so many neglected tenements. Then, once the last few jobs dried up, the inner city was all but deserted. That's when the sectarians came in."

"When was this?" I asked.

"… I can't say precisely," he said, "less than five years ago, by all accounts."

"What is their faith?"

"… I don't know."

"Are they Christian?" I asked. Christian.

"No," he said, "… well, honestly I can't say—I don't *feel* that they are."

"Do they call themselves anything?"

With evident chagrin the young man said again that he wasn't sure, "… Something about 'path' and 'light,' possibly …"

I continued to ask questions, and the young man spoke freely. Although he was clearly very knowledgeable about the history of the town whenever we touched on it, he could give only the most approximate answers to my questions about the sectarians.

"As far as I know, they have no schools—as a matter of fact, I don't think they have any children to send. At least, I've never seen any. Although, their numbers have been growing by all accounts."

"Have they had much success proselytizing here?"

"I've never heard of such a thing. They really avoid almost all contact with us."

"But, if they are celibate, and don't seek converts, how can their numbers have grown?" I asked.

"… I believe they are congregating here … emigrating from other, smaller towns in other parts of the state—and I think I heard something about a few coming in over the state line." He named a few places, whose name I took down.

"How many of them do you think there are?" I asked.

"A few thousand souls, more or less."

From the drift of our conversation, I gathered that the sectarians had all but separated the inner city as their own. I said so, and the young man replied that this separation was apparently what the sectarians wanted. There was almost no commerce between the two communities—in fact, the sectarians printed and circulated their own money among themselves, printed on fibrous grey parchment.

When I expressed my incredulity, he responded more fervently—"That's nothing! They can do whatever they like, really. They all but run this town, at least as much as they care to. They protect themselves. What's more, from what I've heard, they've been taking over all the vice trade here."

"What do you mean?"

"It's common knowledge. Once they arrived, they very quietly took over all rackets in town, sure—gambling, narcotics, prostitution. Without ever partaking or participating themselves, mind you—they never do that, but they all have a hand in it."

I left the historical society in the early afternoon. From where I stood, on the curb beside my car, I could see the inner city as a sort of grey haze in the distance. On an impulse, I drove to its outskirts and parked my car at the filling station, where only yesterday I had telephoned Hennel at the rooming house. Not wanting to get lost, I acquired a current local map at the booth, and then set off on foot into the inner city.

Those narrow lanes had barely closed around me when I realized I had made a mistake. I knew what I was doing and had no intention of turning back, but in less than twenty minutes I was straining, hunched with effort simply to stay on the sidewalk. The pavement was uneven, I stumbled and tripped over its irregularities almost with every other step. Thick weedy clumps hid chinks in the cement, my hell would drop down surprisingly far, jarring me to my teeth. I found myself tiring rapidly. Around me, old wood frame buildings and brick buildings more hideous by disrepair were crowded, almost jammed, together. There were all the features of abandoned and run-down buildings, boards over doors and windows, cracked glass, but added to this was a more disturbing quality of willful negligence, as if this part of the city was there only to be ground into the earth.

Here and there, I would see sectarians, alone or in pairs. The men wore plain shirts with a vertical flap over the buttons and a distinctive band beneath their collars, plain trousers and pointed black shoes. The women wore plain dresses, with grey stockings and pointed black shoes; they wore grey bands around their throats. Invariably, the women wore their hair very long, striking an incongruously luxurious note.

Occasionally, a guilty-looking citizen of the outer city would rush by me, with his or her head down. There was no question of their having come on any speakable business—the shops I passed were more like storefront attics, overflowing with trash. I stopped to peer in one dust-caked window, and saw heaps of rubbish piled on bare, loose-planked floors. I saw disemboweled furniture trailing stuffing and rusting springs, incleansibly tarnished painted frames and pitted, green mirrors, invariably cracked; there were improperly preserved and badly stuffed birds and beasts, dry cracked lips crumpled above

129

brown teeth, horrible colorless plumage fuzzed over with black mold. I stood in the window, scanning the back of the "store," when all at once I noticed one of the sectarians, standing behind a boxlike counter, dimly visible in his grey shirt, motionlessly staring back at me. In the gloom, his features were impossible to make out—the store had no lights. There was only the narrow shaft of sunlight from the open door, swimming with dust thick as plankton.

I went over to the door, but the must of the place would not let me enter; it breathed choking dust on me in thick billows. Suddenly, the man came out from behind the counter and strode smoothly up to the door, his eyes fixed on me. Beaming with malice, grinning hatefully at me, he closed the half-glass door behind the door, visible through the glass like a dummy in a sideshow fortune-telling cabinet, staring triumphantly at me. I did not wait or protest; I went on my way, quickly. I passed what seemed to be a whole street of such "shops."

As I followed the lanes, there were more sectarians on the street; in all of them, I detected traces of some morbid excitement. They moved with a sort of vehemence, with attentiveness. These sectarian faces were bursting with what I can only call evil joy. I had the intolerable feeling of being gloated over as I walked down their streets, these streets that were so clearly theirs.

Walking required too much of my attention, and the closeness of the air made any physical effort a strain, so, impulsively, I hid myself in a steaming alley, where I could watch them undistracted.

In their puritan clothes, with their sprightly steps and bright-eyed alertness, they emanated a palpable air of profound debauchery. I've never seen such carnal people. With every gesture, standing together talking inaudibly on the dilapidated stoop of a sagging house across the narrow way from me, they seemed to be shuddering with little frissons of pleasure—and all the same, there was a hostile, deadening crackle about them, a sickening, dissipated haze in the air. As they passed, emerged from buildings or escaped from view, they seemed to come and go from voluptuous nowhere.

When the group I had been watching slowly and deliberately turned their wide-eyed malicious grins on me, I fled those streets as best I could. They made no move toward me, they had stood where they were and turned to me, as a sign that they had not been unaware of me. Confused, I fled almost in a panic. I haven't had an asthma attack in years, but the dread of one, of one *there*, nearly strangled me, nearly brought one on. The image uncontrollably foisted itself on me—of falling down in those filthy gutters, straining for breath, being surrounded by an unbroken, glaring ring of sectarians, a stifling, pressing ring of wide-eyed grins.

I escaped. In fact, the next thing I knew I was miles away, on the interstate, heading towards home.

What did I know now? There was no doubt in my mind, and there had never been much doubt to begin with, that the sectarians had destroyed Hennel. It is not for me to say how—but why: I knew he had been killed for his work, for having uncovered the figures in the forest. I knew what I had seen and this was certainly enough proof for me.

I insisted to myself that I was not fleeing the sectarians for good, that I was going to serve Hennel's memory by doing my own research, and that I would discover, if only to spite them, what connection there was between the sectarians and the figures Hennel discovered in the forest.

There was no connection. I will say that now, so as not to be too afraid to say it again later. The sectarians and Hennel's figures were not *connected*.

I pursued every record, all existing leads about that town. There was never the slightest mention of the sectarians—not five years ago, not at all. To all accounts, in newspapers and other documents I have traced, the inner city of that town had been only partially deserted; its population had been reduced in the last few years by emigration, but the census results were simply too high to correspond to the depopulated ghost town I had visited. The first mention of the sectarians, of any kind, occurred in a newspaper article dated *the day after Hennel's discovery.* This article claimed that, although no one "quite remembered" when the sectarians had come, that they had certainly been there in large numbers for "some years."

I am thorough. I had taken down the names of those towns from which the sectarians were supposed to have emigrated to join the community in the inner city. I found no record of any sectarians in those towns, no evidence of sectarian communities anywhere, not within hundreds of miles. Using old phone books, I compiled a lengthy roster of the persons who had addresses listed in the inner city, who had been displaced by the sectarians, or who had abandoned the town, at any rate. Out of a list of several hundred people, I was able to trace two. I discovered that many of the names on my list appeared on other lists in other hands—lists of missing persons. I followed as many of these as I could, decidedly the majority, and, in all but a handful, found that the reports dated back no further than a few weeks. Invariably, I found that these cases had either been closed or were simply lying fallow. "Lack of evidence" was the inevitable reason. Yet time and again, in almost every instance, I had the impression that the investigators responsible for these cases had forgotten them, and were somewhat confused when I brought them up. I did not keep count, but in at least a dozen cases, I was told precisely this by the detective, personally: "I'd forgotten all about it." What's more, there was not the slightest doubt in my mind that they would forget again the moment they set the telephone back in its cradle.

There is more—four weeks later, a dream:

I am with Hennel in large empty rooms, no furniture, pale patches on the walls where pictures had hung, loose trash on tile floors. Hennel and I are not finding what we came to find—I have a terrible feeling of concern for Hennel, asking myself "Is he all right? Is he all right?"

I am sitting in a bare white room. Stunningly bright sunlight blares reflected off a white brick wall opposite the windows, sharp shadows. Hennel and I are passing from one cavernous, empty room to another, moving slowly through vast rooms.

On a table in one corner, I see what I somehow know to be Hennel's notes and papers. When I approach to examine them, I cannot find them. Suddenly I step outside through a pushbar exit door into blinding sunlight, through it is the new moon I see hanging in a blue sky. After a brief moment of confusion, I realize I am looking out over the inner city from some high spot.

I experience crashing, total desolation. I turn looking for the car.

"Car? What car?"

I frantically look for Hennel.

There is no car here.

Hennel is not here.

I see the grey haze of the inner city quake. The buildings are gone—horrified, I see sectarians milling in the streets, I see them standing in varying elevations where the buildings once were—and I know that they are not fully revived, fully alive blazing with disappeared souls. I am unable to move. There is a sound of baying dogs in the distance, and something like a cry of many voices raised in dismal triumph. I see the rest of the city vanishing. I can see the historical society, and, through its transparent walls, the young man. I can see the filling station, the hospital, the rooming house. The young man flickers out like a silent film, the city, the people, flicker and shudder beneath the new moon—the sun itself is ebbing—I'm calling, begging them not to abandon me.

There is nothing here.

There is nobody left.

I remember Hennel's voice speaking of the returning ice age of dreams, the time coming and fossilized dreams slowly breaking the surface of the earth, uncovered a little prematurely and emerging still drowsing and trailing illusion until now, their proper time—I understand that this dead wave will ebb then spread, the window of opportunity for dreams that are not human to visit us will *gape*.

Overhead the sun vanishes.

I woke up crying "NO NO NO!"

That morning I was oppressed with the lingering shreds of that dream, which would not leave me. I examined the newspapers: it was the first night of the full moon. The first night of a new moon since the night of Hennel's first telephone call. Lunar cycles—I realized then that I owed my life to the alternations of the moon. When it was strong, however that strength was measured—make no mistake—it had been possible for them to kill Hennel. It had not been possible for them to kill me; I was in the wrong "temporal complexion." Perhaps it was for this reason that what I did was not subject to an illusory lag of "about five years."

I used to rail about "the circle of human firelight" and the "limit of human knowledge."

What is the "limit" of nothing?

I retraced my route. I acquired another car. As I drew steadily nearer my oppression grew in strengthening blows. Traffic thinned out noticeably, until I was alone on the highway. A few dozen yards beyond the rest stop I passed two ambling sectarians—I did not look as I went by, I kept my eyes from the rear-view, I was nearly doubled over the steering wheel. After a few minutes I slowed the car, climbing the shallow rise over which I would catch first sight of the town. I came over the rise and I rolled to a stop; I got out of the car and stood beside it on the empty interstate.

The name of this town will mean nothing to you, even if it was once your hometown—it is not on any map, it cannot be found in any memory, any more. It is no longer a dying town. It is dead forever. I am, most likely, the last person ever to find it; and it was like coming across a corpse lying in tall grass in a lonely place. I recognized nothing familiar in that scene but the inert grey haze of an endless, empty hour, that had spread from the inner city, now hanging down out of a dead sky. A silent, numbing wind rank with the odor of mold blew up from those petrified streets, scattered with useless things. My dream had eavesdropped on their dream, that did this; I had witnessed it as it happened. The only real inhabitants of the town had flickered and gone out one by one, and a blank had been cleared in time, a grave for this town, a dead gap—colonized. Even from a distance, as it sank into its grave, I felt it tug at me.

I felt myself *flicker*.

I was too far away. I was beside my solid car and the hardtop interstate. I held the upper edge of the door tightly with my fingers and insisted on the sensation, the metal, the rubber seal, and the glass. I remained.

Then, I heard a scattering of gravel behind me. The two sectarians passed close by me, on the shoulder. They only stopped after they had gone a few more yards down the road. The man turned to me, and I recognized his face. I had seen it last in a photograph, shining up out of the earth, stirring, becoming aware again. He told me,

"This place belongs to the Gods now."

They resumed walking, slower and slower, towards the town, which was blurring, fading.

I stood where I was, beside my car, knowing everything. All the same, the question framed itself in my mind and burst from my mouth,

"*Who* are the Gods?" I asked them.

The other, a young woman, gave me a look that mingled serenity and viciousness—hard, wild, and quiet—and said … with such sweetness …

"*We* are the Gods."

THE TALES OF INSPECTOR LEGRASSE

H. P. LOVECRAFT & C. J. HENDERSON

Spawned from the classical horror-hunt of Inspector Legrasse,
these seven tales detail an epic confrontation between an
unprepared mankind and the horrors of the Cthulhu Mythos.

$20

The Taint of Lovecraft

by Stanley C. Sargent
Robert M. Price, Editor

The second collection from the author of *Ancient Exhumations*,
Stanley C. Sargent, with wonderful illustrations and
featuring his novella, *Nyarlatophis, a Fable of Ancient Egypt*.
$20

THE LOVECRAFT CHRONICLES

PETER CANNON

From Peter Cannon, author of *Pulptime,*
Scream for Jeeves, and *Forever Azathoth and Other Horrors*
comes three new tales, alternate histories of the Old Gent.
$15

WALTER C. DEBILL, JR.

THE BLACK SUTRA

Nineteen tales of terrors from prehistory
encroaching on the modern world
from Walter C. DeBill, Jr.

$20

Printed in the United Kingdom
by Lightning Source UK Ltd.
122043UK00001B/210/A